speak to my heart

a novel

Stacy Hawkins Adams

Revell
Grand Rapids, Michigan

© 2004 by Stacy Hawkins Adams

Published by Fleming H. Revell
a division of Baker Publishing Group
P.O. Box 6287, Grand Rapids, MI 49516-6287

Second printing, January 2006

Printed in the United States of America

Library of Congress Cataloging-in-Publication Data
Adams, Stacy Hawkins, 1971-
    Speak to my heart : a novel / Stacy Hawkins Adams.
        p.   cm.
    ISBN 10: 0-8007-5970-2 (pbk.)
    ISBN 978-0-8007-5970-4 (pbk.)
    I. Title.
PS3601.D396S68 2004
813'.6—dc22   2004013904

To my mother, Dorothy A. Hawkins,
with all my love

and for

Donald, Sydney, and Donald J,
may you always have faith in your dreams
and trust God to help you realize them.

Moreover he said unto me, Son of man,
all my words that I shall speak unto thee
receive in thine heart,
and hear with thine ears.

Ezekiel 3:10

1

Women and rain don't mix. It's a hair thing, and when the first drops fall, we're often dashing for cover, frantic to protect our 'do.

But three winters ago, as I stood on the banks of the Canal Walk in downtown Richmond, Virginia, with the rain pelting my face and the biting wind piercing my leather coat, I didn't care. I understood for the first time what led some people to kill themselves.

I had never considered myself self-righteous. But that night, I felt like a biblical Pharisee, who for years had been judgmental of others about the right and wrong way to live. I had never seen any gray areas in the Scriptures: Either you followed God's Word to the letter, or you were being disobedient. I didn't beat people over the head with my beliefs, but for me, they were as critical to my existence as breathing.

Do unto others as you'd have them do unto you. Honor

thy father and thy mother. Thou shalt not commit adultery. Yield not to temptation.

Now here I was, the very offspring of false piety. The sins I had pinpointed in others had been shadows in my own life. They had reared up and slapped me in the face.

If the principles in God's Word were so concrete, what happened when we didn't live up to them? What happened when we tried to hide our sins from others so we could appear to be something we weren't, instead of asking for forgiveness?

I knew I wasn't going to jump into the partially frozen river that night, but the shame and the hurt that enveloped me left me wondering how to go on. My heart hurt. I felt as if I'd been hit by an Overnite Express truck crossing the Manchester Bridge at breakneck speed. I felt worthless, even stupid.

How many people had known the truth about my life while I didn't know? How could I not have guessed in all these years? I turned my wet face upward, wishing the answers would drop from the sky with the persistent rain.

The raindrops hit the cold earth and sounded like marbles pinging back and forth in a pinball machine, only at a steadier pace. Somehow, the sound comforted me.

I knelt on the brick-and-concrete pathway that bordered the canal, oblivious to the puddles in the crevices. The moisture quickly soaked the knees of my pants. A sliver of moon escaped the smoky clouds.

I saw, but didn't see, the disheveled man who kept casting looks my way as he shuffled past me, with his ski-cap-covered head slung low. He gripped the rim of a bottle covered by a weary paper bag like it was a cherished possession.

Usually, my senses would have been heightened to danger. I would have quickly moved toward my car. But that dreary night, I didn't budge. I didn't care about whether he would try to hurt me.

Looking back, I can't believe I had ventured into a deserted area of downtown Richmond alone at night. Any other time, at the first sign of questionable characters like this obviously strung-out man, I would have zoomed away in my locked car.

That night, though, my fear-and-flee radar wasn't turned on, or if it was, the alarm was being muffled by the other emotions assaulting my spirit. Whatever I was projecting prevented the man from bothering me. So I knelt there, shivering, and let my thoughts wander. The rain washed away my tears, but not the lead that saddled my heart.

I wondered if I would ever again be able to look people in the eyes with the self-assured focus I'd always had. Despite the challenges I faced growing up with a single, widowed mother, I had never doubted that I was special, that I belonged, that I mattered. But in the short time it took a few truths to cross my mother's lips and reach my ears, that confidence had begun to crumble.

I would always remember that day as the best and the worst of my life.

The pace in the marketing department of the children's software company where I was a long-term temp employee had been hectic. We were preparing for a charity fund-raising gala, and there was much too much to do.

By the time I arrived home, I decided to quickly prepare some stir-fry and spend the rest of the evening doing absolutely nothing. Those plans changed when I checked my mailbox and found a single letter awaiting me. The envelope was thick, so I knew.

Still, when I opened it and read the words inviting me to enroll in Boston University's graduate program in advertising, I couldn't help myself. I screamed a "Thank you, Jesus!" so loudly that the angels napping in heaven must have been startled awake.

The noise led Callie, who lived in the apartment next door, to come over and ask if everything was okay.

I was dialing my mother's work number when I heard Callie's soft tap at the door. I set the cordless phone on the kitchen table and sprinted the few steps to the door. When I opened it, she was standing there, wide-eyed with concern.

Callie, an elementary school teacher who spent most evenings walking her cocker spaniel or grooming her cat, had said little to me in the eighteen months I'd lived next door to her. I chalked it up to her shyness. She rarely made eye contact and generally walked with her head lowered.

I also soon realized that because I was a recent college grad, she had expected me to move in and start hosting loud parties. She thought I was going to be like the women she regularly watched on HBO—the *Sex and the City* crowd with a twentysomething flavor. Or maybe she even ventured to Showtime and watched episodes of *Soul Food* to try to understand me better. I would muse about her musings and laugh to myself.

Shortly after I had unpacked, the assistant manager of

West End Forest had called and asked me to be respectful of my neighbors. She hinted that a concerned resident had sought assurance from her that the unit we lived in would continue to be nice and quiet. Since the only other neighbor on our third-floor level was a single man in his thirties who was rarely at home, it didn't take much detective work to figure out who the "concerned" culprit was.

I hadn't done anything to alarm Callie yet, but she still seemed wary. She'd say hello and glance away, sometimes sweeping a piece of stray blond hair from her eyes when we encountered each other, but offering nothing more. She had seemed surprised to see me leaving dressed for worship service on most Sunday mornings, and I had surprised her again by giving her homemade chocolate chip cookies for Christmas.

But when Callie knocked on my door that winter afternoon and inquired about my scream, I didn't think about any of those things. I was so happy that I hugged her. My words tumbled over themselves as I shared the news of my acceptance to BU, and her green eyes brightened. For the first time, I saw her really smile.

"Good for you, Serena," Callie said and gently patted my arm. "It must be exciting to know your hard work is paying off. When I was a girl in West Virginia, I never dreamed I could go into a field like advertising. Teaching, social work, or being a full-time wife and mother were my safest options."

Callie paused, as if startled by her own frankness. "I love teaching, of course, but it's really nice to see women making strides in other fields."

I squeezed her hand and thanked her for her kind words.

As soon as she left, I dashed back to the kitchen table to call Mama. I sank into the beige sofa, stretched like a cat, and smiled as I waited for her to pick up.

She was at the daycare center, manning the phones as usual. Before she could recite her routine greeting, I blurted out my news.

"Are you ready for an advertising guru in the family, one with a graduate degree from BU?" I asked and giggled.

"You got in!" was all I heard from the other end. I knew what the silence that followed meant. My mother wept when the good cowboy died in old Western movies, at sappy television commercials, and at anything in between. She still got teary-eyed when she talked about the day I was born and my first day of kindergarten.

"Mama, don't cry," I teased. "This is a happy occasion, remember?"

She chuckled but didn't respond. I shook my head and laughed as I waited for her to regain her composure. When she did, her words left me uneasy.

"Baby, I'm so proud of you," she said softly. "Listen, I need to talk to you tonight. Come over for dinner?"

An hour later, I pulled into the driveway behind the cozy brick rancher in North Richmond that I had shared with Mama forever before deciding to get my own place. Mama met me at the back door with a grin that matched my own.

She swung open the door and stretched her arms wide. I fell into her warm embrace and received her squeezes. She was just tall enough for my chin to rest in the crook of her neck. Her familiar smell enveloped me as I leaned into her. She pulled away and kissed my cheek.

When I looked at her, I saw an older, more petite version of myself—smooth cinnamon skin, striking eyes, and high cheekbones that people said made her look regal. Mama's graying hair bobbed at her shoulders, and she was dressed in a stylish, deep purple pantsuit and black pumps. She had obviously rushed home from work and started dinner without changing into something more comfortable.

"I'm so proud of you, baby!" she said, tears dancing on the rims of her eyes. "I knew you'd get in."

Before she could fully close the door behind me, I had unzipped my purse and pulled out the acceptance letter. I danced in place and waved it at her.

"Wanna read it?"

"Of course," she said. I sauntered over to the breakfast nook and took a seat at the round table for two. It still bore the marks of my childhood paint projects and the tic-tac-toe tournaments I often held there with my favorite cousin, Imani. We used notebook paper but wrote so hard with our ballpoint pens that our marks would sometimes leave impressions in the wood whose varnish had long ago worn away.

Mama sat across from me and reached for the letter. Her eyes consumed each word. She seemed to be imprinting the sentences on her brain so she could recite them verbatim when she shared the news with my aunts and uncles and her friends.

Her gaze made me blush when she finally looked at me.

"You've always been one to set your mind to something

and go after it," she said softly, her deep brown eyes locking with mine. "This really doesn't surprise me. It just gives me one more chance to tell you how proud of you I am."

I reached across the table and grasped her hands. She was happy for me, but I could tell she was also jittery.

She stood and demanded that I stay put.

"You don't have to help me tonight, baby. I'm going to serve you."

I threw my head back and laughed heartily. My mother was a trip sometimes. No matter how old I grew, I would always be her baby.

We chatted about nothing in particular over my favorite "Mama-cooked meal": chicken and dumplings, cornbread, and greens—all made from scratch, of course. She even had the nerve after I called her at work to dash home and also make a peach cobbler. We were eating our usual Sunday meal on a Tuesday night.

Later, once she cleared the table and refused my help with the dishes, Mama sat across from me again. She didn't motion for me to join her in the family room, where we usually hung out after dinner to watch TV, play a quick card game, or just catch up on each other's lives.

She sat at the table, tracing the grooves in the wood with her index finger and chatting about how quickly the weather had turned cold. By the time she took a deep breath and looked into my eyes, I knew something was up.

Still, I wasn't prepared for her to wipe my history clean with a few sentences.

"Serena, I've always told you that you can tell me anything, and no matter what, I'll love you."

I nodded slowly and waited for her to continue.

"I hope that works both ways. Sweetheart, it's past time for me to be honest with you about something that will be hard to hear, and harder to say—Herman was not your biological father. Melvin Gates is. I know I should have told you a long time ago, but Melvin and I felt that it was best to keep it to ourselves, for a lot of reasons . . ."

The rest of the evening was a blur. I remember asking Mama to repeat what she said, and I recall her saying that Deacon Gates wanted to pay for grad school. I don't remember saying good-bye to her, leaving the house, or driving to the Canal Walk.

I felt dazed. How could my mother, a married woman with what I had believed all these years was a strong faith in God and an eagerness to live by his Word, have slept with a married man, conceived me, and then lied to me about it my whole life?

For twenty-four years I had been calling the wrong man Daddy and using the wrong last name.

For as long as I could remember, I had visited Evergreen Cemetery to honor the "wonderful man with such a kind heart" who lay in the cold earth and was supposedly my dad. He and my mother had still been married when I was conceived, but what no one bothered to tell me was that for all intents and purposes, they might as well have been divorced around that time.

Mama had alluded to the circumstances on that night when she had made her revelations. I don't remember any details. If she had tried to offer them, I hadn't heard her.

The man I knew as Deacon Gates, a respected and almost revered member of the church I had attended my entire life, was actually my father? As those words had quickly slipped through Mama's ruby lips, like a bad taste she wanted to rid herself of, I thought I would lose my dinner.

Deacon Gates's sons had attended high school with me. I almost dated one of them.

Memories raced through my mind that night as I sped away from Mama's. Deacon Gates had always seemed to take a special interest in how I was doing in school and in my activities at church. He had always given me lingering but inoffensive hugs and a few dollars whenever we crossed paths after service. Now I knew why.

The one thing I do remember doing that night after dinner with Mama was calling information from my cell phone as I drove without really seeing the road. The operator gave me Melvin Gates's home number, and I dialed it immediately, unsure of what I would say if anyone answered.

Mrs. Gates, the soft-spoken petite woman who always wore jazzy hats on Sunday and sat in the same pew three rows from the front in church, picked up on the third ring. It was all I could do to keep myself from screaming the truth in her ear. Or did she already know?

With as much composure as I could muster, I asked for Deacon Gates.

When he said hello, I pulled my Toyota to the side of the road. I was beginning to shake, but I had to do this.

"This is Serena," I said slowly, between clenched teeth. "I know the truth."

He didn't respond. *His wife must be standing nearby,* I fumed. I heard a young girl in the background.

"Daddy, come on, I need you to read my bedtime story. Please?"

Daddy. To Kami, the little girl he doted on and called his special gift from God to anyone who'd listen. When his sons had gone to college, he and Mrs. Gates had begun serving as foster parents. They took custody of Kami when she was six months old and eventually adopted her. I heard her kiss his cheek while I held the phone. Was God twisting this knife in my heart?

Before Deacon Gates—*Daddy Melvin*—could speak, I hung up and tossed the cell phone into the passenger seat.

Minutes later, I found myself on the outskirts of downtown, at the Canal Walk, staring at images of Robert E. Lee and other Confederate heroes. Usually, I'd shake my head at the lack of culture and diversity displayed on the wall just above the James River, but tonight, only the trickling water spoke to me.

The property along the Canal Walk was being developed to offer the city a bustling nightlife venue, but on that night it still was isolated.

I went there intending to pray, but my heart was too bruised. Thoughts raced through my mind so quickly I couldn't keep track of them.

Instead of words, tears flowed.

Come to me, my daughter, and I will give you rest.

For the first time since I'd given my life to God as a teenager, I felt empty. I didn't know what to say to God. Was that really him I heard calling?

I had always been able to pray from my heart. The right Scripture had always surfaced at the right time to comfort or guide me. His Word had been instilled in me since childhood. And I knew from other trying times in my life that his presence was always with me.

But that night, the gentle voice I usually heard so clearly seemed distant. I couldn't put into words what I needed from God, even though he seemed to be speaking to me and seemed willing to help me. I sat there waiting for the words, but they wouldn't come. I remembered that God understands us even when we don't talk, but that night, I felt cut off from his presence.

Somehow, I made my way back to my car. Shivering and damp from the night showers, I turned the heat on full blast, flipped on the windshield wipers, and drove toward home, barely noticing traffic signals or the cars in other lanes. For the first time in what had to be forever, I obeyed the speed limit without forcing myself.

Be still and know that I am God. Give me your burdens. Honor thy father and mother . . . Be still and know—

I knew God was reaching out to me, but I closed my heart. I blasted the music to turn my thoughts elsewhere, even though I wasn't listening to the songs. On that twenty-minute ride to Henrico County, the suburb I called home west of the city, I decided that I didn't want to "turn the other cheek."

How was I supposed to honor a woman who had looked me in the eyes and lied so well for so many years? How was I to honor a man who let me grow up fatherless, while I longed to have a daddy like most of my friends?

I was furious at Mama and at any and everybody who had something to do with this, who knew the truth and helped hide it from me. I even felt a little angry with God.

If serving him all these years has led me to this, what's the point? I bitterly asked myself as I drove more and more slowly. *Why bother?* Even the people I had considered the most spiritual were turning out to be hypocrites.

Singing in the choir didn't matter. Neither did serving as a deacon, one of the church's most trusted officials. Or, apparently, reciting Scripture from memory, as my mother often did.

As I turned off the interstate and merged onto the parkway that led to my place, I decided I needed a break. Right then. From everyone and everything, including my mama. And God.

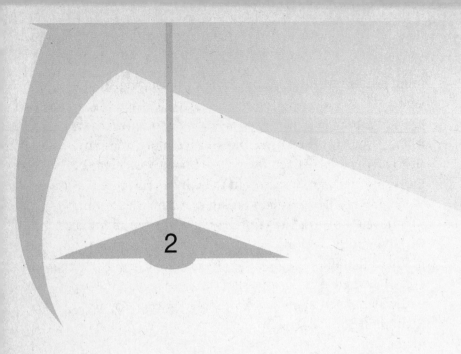

2

As I brushed my teeth and peered into the mirror through still-sleepy eyes, my thoughts drifted back to that February night long ago. Knots formed in my stomach as I remembered my anger and shame and the resolutions I had made.

If nothing else, I was a woman of my word. After years of singing in the St. Mark's Baptist Church choir, helping out in the summers with vacation Bible school, and regularly leading art workshops for the youths at church, I had literally faded away from the congregation after that night.

One day they saw me and poof, the next I was gone.

Pastor Taylor had called when I failed to show up for rehearsals, meetings, or even worship that next month. He said he had noticed my absence and was concerned. The congregation numbered about five hundred, so when one of his active members was missing in action, he quickly touched base with him or her.

Maybe I should have appreciated his taking the time to seek me out and ask if I were okay. Instead, I felt like he was invading my space. I gave him a generic excuse.

"Thanks for calling, Pastor, but everything is fine. I've just been busy."

I used the same line with Farrah when she called to ask why I had missed so many choir practices.

"I know you ain't mad that Stephanie led that song you been singing the solo part on, are you? That kind of stuff usually don't bother you."

Farrah didn't mince words. She handled me and the other choir members like she did her four hyperactive sons, who, like untrained ponies, sometimes needed to be corralled.

I had laughed at her attempts to figure out whether she had driven me away from the church by trying a new voice out on a familiar song. I hadn't been there, but anytime Stephanie opened her mouth, beautiful notes flowed from her pipes. She had probably sung the song better than I ever had, and then some.

"Now, Farrah, God don't like ugly," I had said and laughed. "I didn't write or record that song; I'm not hating. I'm just busy these days. I'll be back eventually."

As soon as I uttered the words, I grew uncomfortable. Was that my conscience nagging me? Did I sound like the hypocrites and liars I now considered my mother and Deacon Gates to be?

I pushed those thoughts aside. Everybody didn't need to know my business. I didn't have to tell Farrah things she'd want to share in the prayer before choir rehearsal.

I could just hear her: "Dear Lord, please be with Serena

as she accepts what we've always known: The reason she looks so much like the Gates family is because she is *part* of the Gates family. Help her to love them and to return home to you, Lord."

The whispering would start before the choir members uttered "Amen."

But as active as I had been at St. Mark's, I knew my sudden disappearance was the subject of some conversations anyway.

Pastor Taylor had eventually called again and left a message on my voice mail, asking me to set up an appointment with his secretary to meet with him. I suspected that Mama had put him up to it. I never responded to his request, and he didn't call again.

It didn't matter much, because by that time I was packing my bags for Massachusetts. Boston University beckoned and provided a much-needed reprieve from Richmond and the façade of normal life surrounding me there.

On the surface, things had seemed fine. I went to my marketing job, shopped for groceries, and hung out with friends from work.

The hours I had, for years, filled by attending services on Sunday and hanging out with Mama and my other relatives afterward now seemed to drag on forever. Sunday had no end. Instead of relaxing at Mama's or Gram's and waiting for my aunts, uncles, and cousins to come by for the dessert of the week, I'd meet some of my younger co-workers for lunch or sometimes a movie. I finally read most of the books that had become a haphazard pile in a corner of my bedroom as the pages waited to be turned.

I went on dates with guys I met in the mall or in a

bookstore, only to be bored within the first fifteen minutes. Either they were players, they had stopped maturing in high school, or they needed personality makeovers. Or if they seemed worth my time, their cell phones would ring in the middle of dinner, and they'd hastily shut them off without checking the number.

Later for that. I had folded the napkin resting in my lap during my date with Carl, a handsome former college football player, and suggested that he take me home so he could call his girlfriend—or wife.

Sometimes I'd give in to my temptation to flip the channel to the Gospel Broadcasting Network. One Sunday I watched the famous Rev. J. D. Hicks mesmerize his congregation with messages from God. Rev. Hicks strutted across his expansive pulpit like a peacock preening before the thousands in his flock, showing them how God could inspire greatness. I was soon glued to the screen, soaking in his words as if I needed to fill an empty fuel tank.

I nodded as Rev. Hicks told the congregation that God was a best friend and a comforter.

It feels so good to be reminded of that, I thought.

Then the cynicism set in.

Anybody can talk a good game. I don't know Rev. Hicks—I didn't even know my own mother. And what kind of best friend lets you live someone else's lie for so long?

The next Sunday, with my tank still on empty, I tried watching the fiery Rev. Joshua Lee. Rev. Lee squinted at the camera and shook his index finger at his congregation, declaring that wrongdoers would suffer for tearing down God's kingdom. This time I didn't even have a few minutes to feel good about the message before the cynicism hit.

There he goes, spouting words, like almost everyone else, I told myself. *I've seen that fiery finger shake before, when Deacon Gates caught his boys kissing girls behind the church, and when Mama scolded me for numerous minor infractions. Sometimes the real wrongdoers are in the back of the finger . . .*

I picked up the remote and turned to MTV. I wasn't going to beat myself up about my decision not to hang out with the holier-than-thou Sunday-morning winners and Monday-morning sinners. Church wasn't going to serve as my aspirin. It couldn't fix what ailed me when the problem was right there, inside the sanctuary.

In Boston, I spent eighteen months immersing myself in campus life and learning as much as I could about advertising. I wanted to be one of the graduates to be reckoned with by the time I left.

I got off to a great start when I landed a summer internship in one of the city's prestigious agencies. My favorite college professor had once been a partner in the agency and had been so impressed with my work that he'd recommended me for one of only three internship positions.

My summer internship at the Cambridge Agency turned out to be important for two reasons. First, I got to work with some of the brightest people in the field and make some valuable contacts for the future. Second, I had a legitimate reason not to return home to Richmond . . . to Mama.

The little time I spent with Mama during grad school occurred during my first Christmas at BU, and the only reason I showed up then was because my dorm closed during the holidays.

When I had arrived that December, Mama had been

uncharacteristically unsure of herself. She hugged me, but she backed off when she realized my response was lukewarm. The strain between us was obvious—as searing as a sudden burn to the finger. Every interaction seemed stiff and involved a formal "please" and "thank you."

I had moved out of my apartment to go to BU, so I was forced to stay with Mama and sleep in the bedroom she and I had decorated pink and white when I was fourteen. I had to use the bubblegum-pink telephone and sleep under the cotton-candy-colored comforter sprinkled with yellow, pink, and white daisies.

On my third night home, Mama had tried to apologize.

As she washed the dishes and I dried them after dinner, we both stood at the sink and stared out of the kitchen window into the inky night, not really seeing much. The silence was thick enough to slice.

"Your Barbies are still in your closet on the top shelf, just waiting to be taken down and dressed to model," she had said teasingly yet with timidity.

She cast a sideways glance at me and kept scrubbing a pot that already seemed spic-and-span. It had been a running joke between us for years how as a young teenager, I would coerce her into playing Barbies with me, long after my friends had put their dolls away for good.

That night, though, I wasn't biting the bait. I shook my head, offering that as a silent "No thanks."

Mama paused and turned to me, compelling me to look at her.

"You know, Serena, we can talk about this. We're two adults. Nothing has changed. I'm still your mother. You're still my baby. I made a mistake—we all do at some point in our lives. Let's talk through this."

For a second I almost relented. The tears welled up in my eyes, and I almost leaned forward to hug her. I almost asked her why this had happened, *how* this had happened, and why she had lied to me for so long. I almost told her how I felt, that I was ashamed to be the product of an extramarital affair, that I felt like I was wearing the scarlet letter she seemed to have so easily tossed aside.

But the memories of that night at the Canal Walk months earlier came rushing back. The memories of the nights I lay awake as a little girl, afraid an intruder might invade my fatherless home, crept in. The frustration of having to ask my uncle to stand in as my escort at my school's father-daughter banquet surfaced.

Anger wasn't far behind. I looked at my mother and felt like I was staring into the eyes of a stranger.

Is this the honest, thoughtful woman with integrity who raised me, or was that just a sham for my benefit? I couldn't help wondering.

How can the mother I loved and was proud to call my own also be this person who fell so deeply into sin and secrets that she waited nearly a quarter of a century to tell the truth, and then did so only for the sake of financial assistance?

The more those thoughts ran through my mind, the less I wanted to talk to her. I shook my head and laid my dish towel on the sink.

"I can't do this, Mama. I'm here for Christmas. That has to be enough right now."

She tried again. "Serena, I'm not perfect. I'm sorry. I know this is a big deal to you, and I understand. But some people never know their fathers. Some people would never know the truth."

I went to my room and lay on my bed in the dark, staring at the ceiling, seeing nothing. The darkness that filled the familiar space seemed to be filling my spirit as well.

Some people may never know their ancestry, I thought, *but I need the anchor of belonging to someone.*

I needed to have a heritage to feel secure in such a shiftless world. I needed to know that my father had left me because he had no choice; not because he was married to someone else and already had a family. I knew Mama loved me, but it hurt to know that the life she had crafted for me had been based on lies. I didn't feel whole without a respectable, explainable history.

But you have me. I can fill you the way a past, present, and future ancestry or pedigree never can . . .

I shut off that voice by forcing sleep.

For the rest of my stay, I spoke to Mama only when necessary. I secluded myself in my room or went out with my former high school or college buddies. I declined to join her at St. Mark's for the Christmas Eve service. I had refused Deacon Gates's offer to help pay for grad school, and I still didn't want to see him or his family.

Mama had prepared all of my favorite Christmas dishes, so we always had food at home for people who stopped by, but every year we ate our big holiday meal at Gram's with all the relatives. Christmas dinner had been tense, but Mama and I tried to be cordial and keep our estrangement to ourselves.

Unfortunately, Aunt Flora's seventh sense—her nosy radar—was working overtime as the family gathered around the long cherry table that Gram and Granddaddy had bought years ago, soon after they married.

Each of us settled in the seats we occupied during every family gathering. Gram sat at one end of the table and Uncle Joe, the eldest son, at the other, where Granddaddy had held court before he died.

Aunt Flora peered at Mama and me through the brown-rimmed glasses that covered most of her face and made her eyes appear larger than life.

"After we bless the food, I'd like to make an iced-tea toast to Serena and Violet," Flora said in her high-pitched voice that always seemed stuck on falsetto. She looked at Mama and me, seated next to each other near the middle of the table, and smiled. "It's just so good to see you two together! Serena, a girl shouldn't leave home to get a fancy degree and forget about her mama!

"Jason would never stay away from me for so long. I remember when he spent a semester in Europe during his junior year at Princeton. He called home every week, and Lester and I flew over twice to see about our baby."

I clenched the napkin in my lap, certain that the expression on my face was more of a grimace than a smile. Mama lowered her eyes to her empty plate and remained silent.

Aunt Jackie coughed, but Flora, in her own bespectacled world, continued.

"When was the last time you were home, Serena? Is graduate school keeping you that busy? I can't believe Violet hasn't made a trip to Boston to see you."

Before I could respond, Mama looked at Flora and said

with a stiff smile, "Flora, Serena is home, we're happy she's here, and that's all that matters. Let's bless the food."

I glanced at my other aunts, uncles, and cousins as we all stood and waited for Uncle Joe to say grace. They were either rolling their eyes at Aunt Flora or looking away in discomfort. I could tell this wasn't the first time most of them had heard her "concerns" about the distance I'd been keeping.

Gram was giving her daughter one of her stern looks, as if saying, "Flora, don't start no mess today . . ."

We all said amen at the end of Uncle Joe's marathon blessing and eagerly sat down to serve ourselves, pretending that nothing had happened.

Even in my stubbornness, I could see that Mama was miserable. She picked over her food and didn't laugh as heartily as usual. Still, something wouldn't let me relent.

No one in the family (Herman Jasper's family, that is, because Mama was from Texas) knew what to make of the tension between Mama and me. They were aware of my extended absence from church. They knew I didn't come home or call Mama as often as I should.

I didn't know what Mama had told them, but thankfully, they didn't pry. After the pre-dinner exchange, even Aunt Flora behaved herself.

I was tempted to blurt out the truth, to give them the shock of their lives as we ate turkey and dressing. But despite my smoldering resentment, I knew better than to lash out. I knew that if I did that, I'd be doing more than just forcing them to look at Mama in a new way. I'd be boxing myself into a shameful corner, too. I'd be letting them all know—both the relatives I adored and the snooty ones who thought they were better than me—that despite my education at BU and a promising, financially rewarding career, I was illegitimate—nothing but a fake.

That Christmas visit to Richmond had been nearly unbearable. Afterward, I had decided I would either stay on campus or go home with my classmates during other holidays.

Shortly before graduating from BU, I returned to Richmond with a recommendation in hand from the Boston firm where I had interned. I landed a position with Turner One Concepts, another top advertising agency that just happened to be based in my hometown. Despite my difficulties with Mama, I didn't mind returning to Richmond after graduation. I knew making work-related contacts and finding mentors would be much easier in familiar territory.

I reconnected with Erika, my best friend from our undergraduate days at Commonwealth University, the local state college in the heart of the city. Erika had just received her real estate license, and since I'd be repaying expensive student loans with much of the largest salary I'd ever received, we both needed a roommate to make ends meet.

In college we'd had our differences, a major one being my faith. Erika had never understood how someone as smart as I was could naively believe in a God I couldn't see or touch. She found the concept of faith alien and considered my commitment to church and various ministries as old-fashioned, something boring people did.

"I couldn't imagine my life without God, Erika," I had explained with a shrug of my shoulders. "He cares about our struggles, our fears, even the friendship you and I share."

My words never seemed to move her back then, and I didn't push her. I always remembered Mama's minisermons about how loving and trusting God were personal choices.

"Jesus never forced people to love him or to follow him," she'd sometimes say when I had questions about our faith. "If you're living as you should, your actions speak louder than your words anyway."

Now, years later, I was thankful for my earlier restraint with Erika, especially since I had pulled back from worship myself. I still prayed to God every so often, mostly out of habit, but I hadn't set foot in St. Mark's Baptist Church since that winter Mama had told me the truth.

I didn't blame God for what had happened, but I questioned how people who claimed to love him and live for him could do such dirt and then keep sinning by lying about it. It was one thing to make a mistake, but keeping it hidden to protect one's appearance of sanctity was hypocritical.

And I knew I couldn't face Deacon Melvin Gates or watch my mother stand before the congregation and read the church announcements with her bright smile and innocent expression. My stomach would have turned.

Erika was right all along, I surmised. *Church is just a social club, and look what it helped create: me.*

I closed my eyes at my reflection in the mirror as those ugly feelings began to surface. I suppressed them and reached for a washcloth to dab at the corners of my eyes before leaning in closer to the mirror to inspect my mess of hair.

I was a week overdue for a perm, and it showed. Grabbing in one handful the lengthy mass, I pulled it up into a ponytail. I twisted it into a chignon that rested at the nape of my neck. It would be that kind of hair day.

I dabbed on lipstick and then a sheer lip gloss and puckered to make sure it was perfect. I quickly brushed blush across my checks and then stepped back for a thorough inspection.

I smiled at myself to make sure there was no lipstick on my teeth and gave myself a final glance. My cocoa complexion, flowing hair, and tall stature often led to compliments, but when I looked in the mirror, all I saw was an average-looking woman with full lips. I still saw a little girl who didn't always wear the right clothes and didn't always feel safe with just her mother, and not a father, to protect her. I shook my head in an attempt to discard those emotions. Time to focus on the present.

I had a meeting with my boss today, and I needed to be in a good frame of mind. I said one of the rare prayers I offered these days. *Lord, be with me. This meeting sounds important.*

I smoothed the lapel of my navy pantsuit, checked my watch, and headed down the hall toward the door.

"Bye, Erika!" I yelled as I grabbed my cashmere cape off the rack beside the door. *Sleeping beauty must still be snoozing,* I thought as I reached for an apple and the last piece of chocolate cake that stared at me from the crystal cake plate on the dining-room table. I had baked it over the weekend when I grew bored with Lifetime and HBO. I had seen all of the movies both channels were showing on Saturday.

A twinge of guilt filled me. If I kept eating like this and missing tae bo and step aerobics, I'd be paying in the hip department soon. I didn't want to think about that today, though. Work was calling me. I was on my way to see Max.

I loved my boss and my job. I never fretted about getting it right or being good enough there. I expected today's meeting to go well. At Turner One, I was on it. Always.

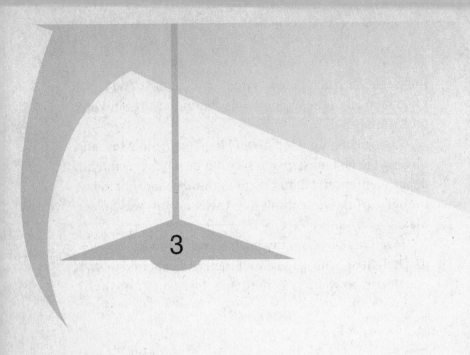

3

I gulped down my makeshift breakfast as I weaved through traffic and flipped from one morning show to another on the radio. Russ Parr was something else, but so were Tom Joyner and his crew. And that Tavis Smiley could make me smile any day.

Turner One was just a few miles from the Shockoe Bottom apartment Erika and I shared. Within minutes, I had arrived at the Main Street office and was perusing the *Times-Dispatch* at my desk, as I did each morning.

As I read the Metro Business section, Hannah, the advertising rep who sometimes worked with me on projects, sat at her desk nearby reviewing her notes for a presentation she had to deliver later that afternoon. Every now and then she'd frown as if she were worried.

"You've got all day, Hannah," I teased her. "Give your brain a break. You can't sit there and read that material over and over until 3:00."

"Why not?" she asked with a serious expression on her face and returned to her task. Before I could respond, my interoffice line buzzed.

"Max is ready to see you," his secretary, Marla, said.

I purposely lingered around my desk for a few minutes so I wouldn't seem too anxious. Then I took the elevator to the so-called penthouse, the elegant suite of executive offices on the fifth floor of Turner One's headquarters.

Max Turner didn't waste time. Minutes after I settled into the burgundy leather chair in his window-encased office, he started talking. "Serena, I'd like you to lead the campaign to land us a multimillion-dollar account with a major airline. Your promotion to senior account manager comes with a corner office and a very nice raise—somewhere in the ten thousand dollar range."

I immediately began biting my tongue to keep a scream of excitement at bay. I didn't want him to know how badly I wanted what he was offering—that might work against me.

"We didn't have to think long and hard about this because you were our first choice," Max said as I smiled confidently and tried not to squirm with excitement. "With Myra leaving our team to start a consulting firm, we knew immediately that your skills and expertise would be perfect for the job. When would you like to start?"

He leaned back in his chair and made a teepee with his fingers as he waited for me to respond.

"Wow, Max." I sat up straighter and gripped the palm pilot resting on my lap.

Accepting the assignment would mean spending the next three months directing the creative team for a new national campaign for Aviator Airlines, once the second-largest airline in the world. After the September 11 terrorist attacks, the airline had lost millions. The plan was to put a new advertising campaign to work restoring consumer confidence so the airline could regain its coveted position and possibly have more leverage in the industry.

I finally responded.

"This certainly is a surprise—and a great opportunity, Max. What can I say?"

"This new assignment comes with perks," he said and smiled, clearly not expecting a no. He ran his fingers through his sandy blond hair before sitting up and resting his arms on his expansive desk.

"You'll receive a healthy travel budget, Myra's office, which I think has the best view in the building, and an additional week of vacation once the airline signs with us. Turner One Concepts is forward thinking, Serena. We like to promote our best and brightest, and you definitely fall into that category. We consider our employees family, and in your tenure here, you've done a wonderful job. So when should we formally announce this?"

This was the offer of a lifetime. How many young black women held middle-management positions in one of the hottest advertising firms in the country, especially in conservative Richmond, Virginia, the notorious capital of the Confederacy?

Mama would be thrilled, I thought before I could censor myself. Before I'd reached thirty, I was headed for the major leagues.

But this isn't about Mama, I reminded myself. This was all about me and how good I was at what I did. How could Deacon Gates not want to have a daughter like me?

Will the new responsibilities, the raise, and the beautiful office make you happy? Will you be a better servant to me?

I ignored that soft voice yet again. Still clutching my palm pilot, I eased up on my teeth and smiled. Max was looking into my eyes and smiling. Could he see into my soul? Could he read the confusing thoughts swirling through my brain?

"Max, this is a wonderful opportunity," I finally said. "I'm honored that you've asked me. Give me a night to let this sink in, okay?"

He nodded and began searching through a stack of papers on his desk.

"We'll shake on it in the morning."

He knew he was offering me a career-propelling promotion. And I was ready. I'd give this job everything I had, even if it meant sacrificing the next three months of my life, I decided.

As hard as I tried, I couldn't hold back my smile.

"On second thought, I don't need the extra time," I told him. I stood and extended my hand. "Consider me ready to give the job my all. We'll soon have Aviator Airlines as one of our clients."

Max stood and shook my hand. He covered it with his other hand. "Get ready to hustle," he said matter-of-factly. "This campaign is going to move us in a new direction if—no, *when*—we land the account."

I got the message. I was being given a chance, and I'd better not drop the ball.

"I'm up to the challenge, Max," I told him confidently. "I won't let Turner One down."

He chuckled. "I don't expect you to."

4

I left Max's office wanting to share my good news with someone, but found myself out of luck.

Mama used to be the first person I called, but that hadn't been the case in what now seemed like forever. The last time we had really celebrated had been when I was accepted into Boston University. Her tears then had touched me.

More and more, our closeness seemed like something I had manufactured in my imagination. Had it been real? Or was it an illusion, like my devotion to a deceased father who had never really been mine to claim?

Was my relationship with Mama one that worked only as long as we didn't move past surface issues like dinner, job promotions, and the weather? When shadows shifted and the truth reared its head, our bond hadn't seemed as strong. If it had been authentic, there wouldn't have been a need for secrets.

Still, sadness surged through me as I remembered how she used to be a priority on my "must call" list. Sometimes she was the only one on the list, and she had been enough.

My fingers hovered over the telephone keypad. I still knew her number at work by heart. Then I remembered the last time I'd called her to share good news. That day had ended with her revelation. *Who knows what I would learn if I talked to her now,* I told myself.

Instead, I called Erika at her office. She didn't answer, so I punched in a different set of numbers. Still no luck. Her cell phone went straight to voice mail.

She was probably out trying to sell a house. Maybe she would have some good news of her own to share tonight.

Twiddling my thumbs, I looked Hannah's way, hoping she would raise her eyes. I stopped just short of blurting out the news. She might not appreciate me landing such a major account while she was still struggling for more recognition within the agency. She was diligent and did good work, but so far she hadn't been able to secure a spot on one of the teams that handled our biggest clients.

Renae, my exercise buddy at the downtown YMCA, must have been busy working, too. I hung up in frustration after repeatedly trying to reach her and getting her voice mail. I hadn't seen her in a while anyway. Lately, we had spent more time exercising our mouths during our telephone conversations than working on any other body parts.

I hadn't had a serious relationship in more than a year,

so there was no "significant other" to call. The guys I dated occasionally weren't worth taking the time to call.

What was a girl to do? I sighed and decided to call my grandmother. She cooed over the news and asked me several times what it meant.

"So you're in charge of an office project now? Are you one of the bosses?"

I laughed. "Not quite, Gram, but thanks for having so much faith in me. I'm gonna run now, but I love ya."

"Okay, baby," she said in her sweet, Southern drawl. She had lived in Richmond for fifty-two years, but the Alabama accent she inherited at birth remained. "Two things before I hang up: First, you need to get on your knees and thank the Lord for this blessing. And I'm not just saying that. You young people think you get all this stuff and do all these wonderful things on your own, but you've got to give God his due. He is good, baby."

I didn't even roll my eyes because I knew she was right. *I didn't used to need her to tell me those things,* I mused. *It used to be a reflex for me to talk to God, to thank him and praise him. Until—*

"And then," Gram continued, "you need to call your mama, Serena. She needs to hear this good news from you. She won't tell me what happened between you two, but whatever it was, that's water under the bridge. You only got one mama, and she only got one baby. You two need each other."

I handled Gram's speech with the silence I'd become so accustomed to employing. I didn't want any more thoughts of my mother or Deacon Gates to ruin this perfectly fine afternoon.

I crossed my fingers behind my back before I told Gram my boss was calling me.

"Yes, dear, you run on," she said. "But you remember what I said. And I love you."

I sat at my desk and tried to appear productive for the rest of the day, but I was really too excited to focus on any other work. I kept trying to reach Erika, and we began a game of phone tag. As soon as I'd get a business call, she would call and have to leave another message. We finally made dinner plans through voice mail.

That evening as I drove to my favorite soul food restaurant in the Jackson Ward section of the city, Gram's words rang in my ears: *You only got one mama.*

"I know that!" I said aloud as I weaved in and out of the snail-paced traffic. "But what kind of mother is she?"

Honor thy mother, came that soft, compelling voice.

I pushed the voice away, along with the image of Mama's sad eyes the last time I'd seen her, when we had crossed paths in the mall on a crowded Saturday. We had hugged stiffly, with Mama holding on to me longer than I cared.

"How've you been?" she had asked brightly, clutching her two bags and smiling as if being in my presence was making her day. She seemed thinner, but my eyes didn't linger on her long.

I glanced around as if looking for someone and answered her question with a formal response.

"Very well, thank you. And you?"

She got the message. The wall between us wasn't crumbling.

"Well, it's good to see you, Serena. Don't be a stranger," she said, trying to control the tremble that was causing her voice to waver. "Call me or come by sometime. Your key to the house still works."

With that, she had squeezed my hand and smiled.

"I know, Mama," I said before sliding my fingers from her grip.

Erika, who was with me, curiously watched the exchange. I had never told her why I was so angry with Mama.

The few questions she had asked told me she suspected it had something to do with my father, but she wasn't sure what, and she never pressed me. I was grateful that I didn't have to come up with some elaborate, false explanation for her.

Still, she chided me for my response to Mama that day.

"Serena, what's the deal? She's your mother. In all the years I've known both of you, I've seen and heard enough to know that she loves you. I don't know why you've shut her out, but she is so sad. I know you've got to be sad too underneath this tough role you're playing. What gives?"

I wasn't about to make a shocking confession in the middle of Regency Square Mall. I shrugged my shoulders and started walking.

"I don't want to get into it, Erika. Let's talk about it another day."

Of course Erika never brought it up later, so that other day hadn't come yet. And tonight was going to be all about sharing good news.

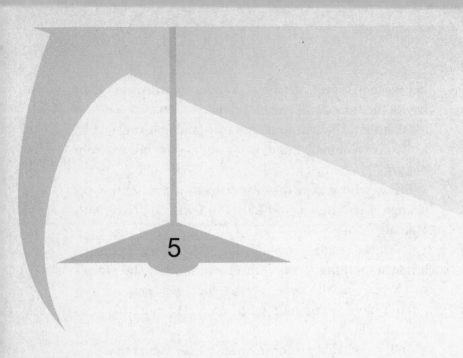

5

Even without the excitement of my promotion, tonight was going to be special. Erika had agreed to meet me at Mister P's as soon as she could leave the office. I was excited that she was coming without Elliott, who stuck so closely to her these days that Erika seemed to have grown an extra limb. We were going to have a bona fide girls' night out. I couldn't wait to share the details of my meeting with Max.

When I arrived at the restaurant, Danielle, the perky waitress with the tightest dreds I had ever seen, led me to my usual table in the rear of the restaurant. Even though it was Wednesday, the place was crowded, as usual.

I snaked through the snugly situated tables, ignoring the minute-too-long stares from some of the men seated at the bar. A fine brother to my left, sitting with a sister whose back was to me, gave me the once-over. He smiled slyly. I wanted to call him out; instead, I looked away.

I couldn't stand guys like that, but I was beginning to realize that the have-it-all-together, no-nonsense image I projected with my professionalism was extending past work hours and costing me. The men I *wanted* to meet seemed afraid to approach me.

I was sure that my straightforwardness, coupled with my hectic job, had something to do with my going without a date for so long. Three months seemed like an eternity, especially since I lived with Erika, who went out every other night with Elliott.

Between working, spending time at the gym, and hanging out with friends from the office or my advertising networking group, I didn't have time for dating men who weren't ready to commit—or more likely, were already involved with someone.

And even though I hadn't faithfully studied God's Word or prayed regularly in a long time, it bothered me that most of the men I did consider dating rarely set foot inside of a church or cracked open a Bible. At least those were the reasons I used to soothe myself. Mama had always scolded me for getting so wrapped up in my work and with my friends that I didn't live my own life. Anyway.

I slid into my chair and smoothed the linen napkin across my lap in preparation for the soda and appetizer Danielle would soon bring. I knew I would order the same meal as always, but I browsed through the menu as I waited for Erika. I expected her to be about ten minutes late, as usual, so I had time to get comfortable.

Danielle slid a ginger ale in front of me, and I turned toward the band. My head bobbed to the rhythm as the group riffed through a set of my favorite jazz numbers from Miles Davis to Cyrus Chestnut.

I giggled when I looked toward the door and saw Erika coming toward me, getting quite a bit more attention than I had from the men in the place. With her petite frame, honey complexion, and hazel eyes, she certainly turned heads. Even years after her graduation, one could see why she had been voted her high school homecoming queen and then Miss Commonwealth University our senior year in college.

Miss Thang floated through the crowd as if she didn't see the men but knew she deserved their attention. Her expression seemed to say, "Look, but don't touch." I shook my head at the scene.

"Hey, girl," she said as she set her purse on the chair next to her and settled across the table from me.

Danielle appeared with a second ginger ale for me and with Erika's regular drink of choice, cranberry juice. Erika surprised both of us.

"Hey, Danielle, turn it up a notch tonight," she said, indicating that she wanted vodka with just a splash of the juice. Erika didn't look my way but gave the waitress a big smile.

Danielle put a hand on her thick hip and didn't try to mask her shock.

"Well, awright! I guess there's a first time for everything," she said before turning on her heels and sashaying away to fill the order.

I raised an eyebrow. What was up? Erika knew I had issues with people drinking and driving. She didn't drink

44

much in the first place, but whenever she felt the urge, she usually did it at home.

She knew that Herman, the man she still thought was my father, had been killed in a head-on collision with a drunken driver when I was eight months old. He was only thirty-seven.

Usually I would have set her straight about the drinking and driving, but I could tell that tonight my lecture wouldn't make a difference. Whatever had led her to order that drink was obviously more pressing than my disapproval.

"Don't give me that look," she said as she sipped on the cranberry juice Danielle had left on the table while going after Erika's new beverage.

"I've had a rough day, and I just need to relax."

The mahogany chair swallowed Erika's miniature frame, but as usual, her feisty manner revealed that she wasn't fragile. I decided to refrain from picking a fight. There was important news to share.

Erika patted her swept-up hairdo with her manicured fingernails and straightened the shoulders of her tailored black jacket as she waited for our buffalo wings to arrive. We always ordered a plate of those before dinner to start off our night filled with music and chitchat.

Before I could launch into the details of my career-propelling promotion, Erika began recounting the particulars of her day, sharing how she had sold one house, shown three others, and landed two potential new clients.

"I'm loving real estate. It's really me," she said. She had studied for her license twice before passing the test and had left her job as an insurance claims adjuster to pursue this new career full-time about a year ago.

"I get to work outside the office, see beautiful homes, and help people get into those homes to live happily ever after. What could be more rewarding?"

If things are going so well, I asked myself silently, *then why do you need the vodka?*

My answer appeared at her shoulder seconds later. Without my noticing, Elliott had slithered into the restaurant to join us for dinner.

Erika's body visibly tensed up as he stood behind her chair and rested his massive hands on her shoulders. Elliott was reed thin, but he was tall enough to be a basketball player. I greeted him coolly.

"Elliott," I said and tried to smile. I was certain it looked more like I had a toothache than anything. "This is a surprise."

Erika hadn't told me he was coming. She knew I had expected it to be just the two of us, giving us a chance to catch up with each other outside of the apartment—and without her hovering, possessive boyfriend. I had wanted her uncensored assessment and celebration of my promotion.

When we were alone, I was used to hearing whatever was on Erika's mind roll off her tongue, with no hesitation or apologies. But that side of her seemed nonexistent when Elliott was around.

He leaned over and kissed her lightly on the cheek. She tentatively looked up at him, then glanced at me, apologizing with her eyes.

"Hi, sweetie, have a seat," she said to him. "I didn't know you were coming out tonight."

His laugh was phony. "I like to surprise you, baby. You never know when or where I'll show up, do you?"

She smiled and nervously began twisting her cloth napkin. She took a sip of her drink and looked down at her lap. My thoughts turned to the last time he had surprised her, during a bachelorette party for one of our girlfriends from college.

Just as Whitney was preparing to open her gifts, we'd heard a rustling outside the window of her first-floor apartment. The blinds were partially open, and night had fallen. We thought maybe a cat or dog was scratching outside.

One of the guests got up to peek outside and looked right into Elliot's eyes. He had been crouched near that window for who knows how long, watching to make sure Erika was behaving herself.

The girl at the window screamed when she realized a man was crouching there.

"Call the police! I think there's a Peeping Tom!"

Elliott raced to the door and yelled for Erika just as I reached for Whitney's cordless phone to dial 911.

"Erika, it's me, Elliott. I came by because I need to talk to you for a few minutes. It's an emergency."

I paused with the phone in middial. Even though I recognized Elliott's voice, I wanted to call anyway.

Erika nearly turned red as she rose from the floor where we were sitting around Whitney. She opened the door.

"He says it's an emergency—sorry, ladies," she mumbled.

When she stepped outside, we could hear raised voices

and a muffled discussion on the other side. I knew that no matter what story Erika gave us when she returned, Elliott wanted nothing more than to keep tabs on her. He wanted her to know that he was watching her every minute.

Instead of coming back inside with an elaborate excuse for the interruption, Erika had returned for her purse.

"Whitney, I'm so sorry, but I have to run. Elliott is having a problem right now that he needs my help with, and it can't wait. I hope you understand."

We were all good enough friends that we usually said what was on our minds. Whitney didn't mince words.

"Elliott can't wait another hour, Erika?" she asked. "I'm hoping to get married only once and to have a bachelorette party and shower just once. Can't he let you stay a little longer?"

That question had let Erika know that we all knew the deal. This intrusion by Elliott was a power play. The question was, would she give in or stand up to him?

"I have to go, Whitney," Erika had said in resignation. "It's just easier this way, believe me. But I'll call you tomorrow and catch up on all the fun I missed and see if you need any other help to be ready for the wedding next week."

With those words, Erika had opened the door and walked away with Elliott, who was standing outside waiting with his back turned to us.

Whitney continued opening her gifts, but I could tell that everyone wanted to talk about Erika's situation. They gave me questioning looks because they knew Erika and I were roommates. But I reminded them it was Whitney's special night.

"Erika's gone, so let's pick up where we left off. At least we didn't have to call the police," I said in as lighthearted a tone as I could muster. Beneath my enthusiasm however, I was simmering—at Elliott for having the nerve to ruin Whitney's party and at Erika for letting him get away with it.

Tonight though, as Elliott acted like dinner at Mister P's had been his fabulous idea, I tried to quash similar feelings. Elliott pulled out the chair next to Erika. Without looking in my direction, he extended her purse toward me to put in the seat next to mine. He sat without even noticing that I was glaring at him as I took the purse. I picked up a menu, resigning myself to the fact that he was staying for dinner.

"I'll have the pork chops," Elliott told Danielle when she arrived with the buffalo wings and asked for our dinner selections. He loosened his tie and put his arm around Erika's shoulders.

Erika refused to make eye contact with me. She knew I was angry because she didn't have the guts to tell Elliott that the two of us had planned to hang out alone. Knowing their relationship, I believed that he really hadn't told her he was coming. I knew she'd ask for my forgiveness later. I decided to try to be nice.

As we ate in silence and listened to the band, I had to grudgingly acknowledge Erika's and Elliott's presence as a pair. Sitting there close to each other, even with Erika's tense smiles, they looked like they belonged together.

The two did make a lovely couple, Erika petite and pretty, and Elliott, nearly a foot taller, with the same honey complexion and a handsome, chiseled jawline.

With one a fast-rising corporate lawyer and the other a successful real estate agent, they could be considered the Cliff and Claire Huxtable of the twenty-first century. With a few years of marriage and then several little ones running around, they could be *The Cosby Show* encore in the making.

But looks really could be deceiving. For the longest, I had tried to impress that upon my friend. Instead, Erika continued to delude herself into thinking that this pleasing picture they painted was reality.

As we shared the wings, Erika glanced at Elliott every so often. She wanted to say something, I could tell, but she wasn't sure how it would be received.

When our meals arrived, I bowed my head and quickly blessed my food. Elliott squirmed in his seat and looked around to see if anyone was watching. He and Erika dug in without following suit. *If he hadn't been here, she'd have at least respected my prayer by bowing her head,* I thought resentfully.

"For someone who has forsaken church, you still can give a sho-nuff good prayer," Elliott joked when I finished my brief offering of thanks.

Come to me and I will give you rest. . . . Why have you forsaken me?

Even in my distraction tonight, that small, still voice seemed to be present.

I haven't forsaken you, God, I argued silently as I dug into my roasted chicken and watched Erika wolf down her ribs. For a little thing, that woman could eat.

Not you, Lord, my internal conversation continued. *It's just those hypocrites in church. How can they lead me? How can*

I be around their fakeness on Sundays when I know what many of them are about the rest of the week?

Keep your eyes focused on me, Serena. Focus on the blood of the Lamb, your Savior, Jesus.

I shut off the inner voice by sharing the news about my promotion. Even with Elliott here, I had to talk about it.

"I'm about to move up to the penthouse," I said and laughed. I spent the rest of the night filling them in on the details of my new assignment.

"It will definitely mean more work, which will limit my free time, but for the prestige—and the raise—I think it's worth it," I said.

Elliott shrugged and slid his chair closer to Erika's, sending a message to other men in the restaurant who might be watching. "What's more important than a great job with good money?" he said nonchalantly. "That's why we're all in this rat race, right? I'm on target to make partner at the law firm soon, so I see the value in getting paid."

Erika smiled in agreement with his assessment but remained oddly silent. She usually had opinions to spare.

"I say go for it, Serena. It's a great promotion," she finally said.

Elliott, though, couldn't say enough, mostly about himself.

"I mean, we're educated black professionals who have worked hard to get everything we have. We deserve the best jobs with rewarding salaries and the nice offices. We deserve to move up the career ladder. I'm doing everything I can now to ensure that nothing stands in the way of my making partner. They'll have no reason not to add my name to the list within another year."

I could see that Erika loved him as she listened to him brag. She was really proud of all he had accomplished.

"And just think," she'd often say to me, "he wants to take me along for the ride. He could have anyone he wants, but I'm the one."

I bit my tongue to keep from saying something I'd regret. "Thanks for sharing your perspective, Elliott," I said politely. "I know that God opens doors for us and helps us achieve many things that within our own power would be impossible."

The God comment silenced him. He stared at me blankly before turning to Erika.

"Is your roommate turning into an evangelist again?" he said and nudged her as he chuckled. "We've got to get you out of that apartment before you get converted. I can't have my future wife trying to be a preacher."

Erika's adoring gaze turned fearful again as she tried to determine whether he was serious. Would he really force her to move out of the apartment with me? Would she let him do that?

I excused myself and went to the bathroom. I wanted to scream once I got there; instead I stood in the corner for a few minutes and took a few deep breaths.

Why was I letting Elliott's presence make me so angry tonight? Part of it, I knew, was watching Erika take his stuff. Nobody else could tell her what to do; she was her own woman. But Elliott barely had to utter a peep and she literally jumped.

Sometimes I wanted to shake her in frustration. But I was determined to keep my emotions in check tonight. I looked in the mirror and took a few more deep breaths before swinging open the door and returning to the table.

Later, as we pooled together a tip for Danielle and stood to leave, Erika said what I realized had been on her mind most of the evening.

"Elliott, I know you would love for me to have such a great opportunity," she said, referring to my promotion. "Then you wouldn't have any excuse for not treating me better. And you wouldn't have to follow me around during your lunch break while I'm trying to sell real estate."

She laughed, but she and I both knew it wasn't a joke.

Elliott didn't think her remark was humorous either. He cut his eyes at me to gauge my reaction.

"Very funny," he said to Erika as he smiled. It was accompanied by a bone-chilling stare. "You know you're my little princess."

Erika nodded and chuckled nervously.

"I'm your black Barbie, and you're my Ken doll, baby."

Lord, please deliver me from la-la land, I prayed as we walked toward the restaurant's exit.

As I prepared to push through the door, someone called my name. I turned to see Tawana, one of the young girls I had mentored at St. Mark's, strutting toward me. I hadn't seen her since I'd left Richmond for Boston more than four years ago.

"Tawana!" I said and hugged her.

"Hi, Serena," she responded, breathing heavily from her light jog across the restaurant. "I thought that was you. I haven't seen you in so long."

I let the twinge of guilt roll off.

"How've you been? And what are you doing in here

so late on a school night?" I asked. Then I noticed her attire.

"I'm on the kitchen staff here," she said. "I work three nights a week after school, cleaning tables and washing dishes. Did you ever get that big-time degree? When you left St. Mark's to go to Boston, I stopped going to church that often. Somehow the youth activities weren't the same without you there."

I smiled and gently touched her shoulder.

"You always were a sweetheart," I said. "But you know I shouldn't be your excuse for not going to church. No one should keep you from worshiping and serving God."

Erika coughed behind me as I spoke. I figured it was her way of letting me know she couldn't believe my hypocrisy.

"Are you back at St. Mark's?" Tawana asked. "Now that you're back, I guess I could come sometime. Maybe we could even go together."

My mouth felt dry. How was I going to tell this child that I hadn't been to church in years myself?

Tawana had participated in the youth art group I had led at St. Mark's and had adopted me as her big sister soon after we met. I had encouraged her to keep doing well in school and to look beyond the hopelessness that was just as prevalent in her neighborhood as drugs and crime. I promised her that if she would stay focused and make the right choices, someday the life she always dreamed of would be her reality.

On the Sunday she was baptized, I sat next to her mother in church and wept. It felt so awesome to be used by God to reach someone else, to show someone else the wonder of God's love. After the service, Mama and I had taken the two of them to dinner at this very place.

Tawana had really admired me. But when I left St. Mark's after the pain and frustration of my mother's revelation, I lost contact with her, too. I had given her my address and phone number in Boston, but grad school was intense. We wrote each other infrequently. When she called, I usually wasn't home. I was too wrapped up in my own drama to call her back as often as I should have.

Eventually we drifted apart, and she had shifted off my radar. I knew she must've felt hurt by this. One more person had abandoned her.

As she beamed at me tonight, waiting for me to fully embrace her and tell her things hadn't changed, I could see that it was my fault.

"You know," I stumbled, struggling to find a legitimate response, "my job keeps me so busy I haven't had time to get back to St. Mark's like I should. But when I do visit there, or maybe even another church, I'll give you a call."

The light in her eyes dimmed. She had been given false promises before, from me and from many others. She knew a line when she heard one.

Still, she pulled a pen out of the pocket of her black slacks and scribbled her home number on the top sheet of her order pad.

"Whenever you have time, Serena. I started working here two days after my sixteenth birthday last month, so I know how hectic things can get," she said. "But I'm still making straight A's and trying to prepare myself to become a lawyer."

She smiled confidently as she spoke. From what I knew of her background, I figured she deserved to be proud. Her mother worked twelve-hour shifts at a local factory, and Tawana had never met her father. None of her other relatives, at least the ones she spoke of, seemed as concerned about education. Of the three cousins close to her age, the two boys had been in and out of juvenile detention before I left for Boston. And the girl had been beginning to skip school. I could only imagine where she was now. I didn't want to ask.

I squeezed Tawana's arm and gave her a hug. "That's no simple accomplishment, Tawana. I'm really, really proud of you. Let's do try to keep in touch."

I gave her my business card with my home number on the back just as I heard Elliott release a loud sigh. I turned to find him and Erika standing near the door, waiting to walk out with me. I couldn't bite my tongue any longer.

"Trying to be a gentleman by waiting for me, Elliott?" I said, my words dripping in sarcasm. "Don't hurt yourself."

This man always seemed to bring out the worst in me. He held the door open for me but didn't say anything. He knew that, unlike Erika, I wasn't afraid of him.

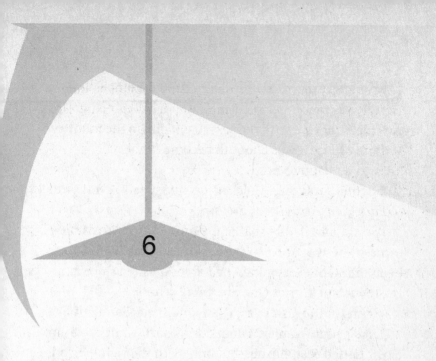

6

In the parking lot, Elliott, ever the gentleman, walked me to my car and waited for me to unlock the door. Then he grasped Erika around the waist and strolled with her toward her car. I started the engine and tapped the button that made my window silently slide down.

"See you at home?" I asked Erika, hoping that she planned to turn in tonight without an episode with Elliott.

She looked at Elliott before nodding at me and getting into her car.

"I'm exhausted," she said. "And I have to finalize a contract on a house first thing in the morning. See you in a few minutes."

The events of the day flashed through my mind as I cruised onto the interstate and put in my Stevie Wonder *Definitive Collection* CD. I hadn't listened to it in a long time. I turned up the volume and laid my head against the head rest as I drove.

I couldn't have been prouder of my accomplishment. Here I was, about to head up a major ad campaign for Aviator Airlines, one of the best companies in the industry. With my help, it was about to become *the* best.

I was so happy, yet . . .

I sighed loudly and picked up my speed. Even with today's good news, I felt hollow.

Was it that I hadn't shared my promotion with Mama? I knew she would be so proud. In fact, she would have been proud of everything I had accomplished since landing the job at Turner One after grad school.

Was it that I wasn't dating anyone special and felt like all I had was my career? I didn't think so. I wanted to be in a committed relationship, but only with the right person. I had never been one to believe that I couldn't be truly happy unless I had a man in my life. Erika's situation had shown me that sometimes relationships could bring more troubles than blessings.

I turned off the music and drove in silence. Alone with my thoughts, I knew what was missing.

Knock and the door shall be opened. Seek and you shall find.

My sporadic connections with God weren't enough. It had been too long since I had immersed myself in my faith, talking to God just because, not when I needed or wanted something.

I knew I couldn't go back to St. Mark's right now; I wasn't ready. But that didn't mean I couldn't find somewhere to fellowship and to serve God with the gifts he had given me. I had too much to be thankful for to keep staying away.

I uttered a dry, ironic laugh. *Funny,* I thought, *how I used to criticize my friends who made excuse after excuse about why they didn't go to church.*

They considered it entertainment. The people there were phony, they said. Church was primarily a meat market for those who wanted to scope out members of the opposite sex, hear good music, and spend time with their friends while *appearing* to be holy.

And now, here I was in that number, avoiding church for those very reasons. Who could have known?

But tonight, after what had been one of the most exciting days in my life, I knew I needed to give thanks to the One who had made it happen. I knew I needed to pray for God's presence and his direction as I tackled this important project.

I don't want your lip service or twenty-second gratitude, Serena. I want all of you. I want your whole heart.

"I hear you, Lord," I whispered.

That was a tall order, especially when part of my heart still held hurt at Mama and felt I-don't-know-what toward Melvin Gates. I had issues, for sure.

But I knew it was time to think about coming home. With God back in my life, I knew everything would be easier to handle, including day-to-day life, and especially work.

For now, though, my thoughts turned to the Aviator Airlines campaign as I drove, and I began to brainstorm ideas.

I should take a couple of flights on the airline to gauge the quality of service and ease in travel, I mused. I needed to review the airline magazines and other entertainment provided to passengers and also sample the snacks distributed during domestic flights.

Customer satisfaction surveys needed to be created and distributed, and I needed to find out if the airline already had a mission statement. If so, that could help me come up with a catchy slogan or brand for the company.

I was so caught up in my mental planning that I had to swerve onto the exit I usually took to get home. I slowed just enough to make the curve but not quite enough.

I didn't see the dark Jeep in front of me at the red light until a second too late. The sound of my Camry touching the bumper of the SUV made me wince.

"Not toniiiiight!" I wailed and laid my head on the steering wheel.

Lord, please let me not have damaged this person's car too much, I prayed silently.

I raised my head and found myself peering into the eyes of a handsome stranger.

"You okay in there?"

Did Denzel Washington have a first cousin about ten years his junior, who, lucky for me, just happened to live in Richmond?

I nodded at him that I was fine. I wanted to get out and survey the damage to the cars, but given the late hour and the secluded intersection, I thought better of it. I slid my window halfway down instead.

"I am so sorry," I began. "It's been a long day, and I wasn't paying attention like I should have. Is there a lot of damage?"

The man raised his hand to shush me.

"It's okay. It's dark out here, but I don't think you did too much damage, at least not to my car. Your bumper may be in worse shape than my bumper. But we can just exchange information and contact our insurance agents."

"Thank you so much," I said and sighed. "I hope you're right, that there's little damage."

He strode to his Jeep to retrieve his insurance agent's number and something to write on.

I would have to hit somebody tonight, I thought, still shaking my head at my carelessness.

He returned with a slip of paper bearing his name, home number, and other pertinent insurance information. I gave him my insurance information and my phone number at the office.

"Thanks, Ms. Jasper," he said, his voice resonating. "Don't worry about this. Things happen."

He flashed me a Colgate smile, and I smiled back weakly.

"Thanks, um . . ." I glanced at his information. "Mr. McDaniels."

He shrugged as if to say "No big deal," and turned to walk back to his Jeep. "If we ever meet again—hopefully under better circumstances—you can call me Micah."

The light had changed several times since we'd been sitting there, but now it was red again. I was chiding myself as I drove away, but I had to smile when I heard strains of India Arie floating through Micah's open window. This man must be all right. She was one of my favorite artists too.

7

By the time I had brushed my teeth, wrapped my hair, and exchanged my pantsuit for my favorite pair of purple silk pajamas, Erika had turned off the light in her bedroom. *She couldn't be asleep that fast,* I thought as I walked toward her door. And besides, I wanted to tell her about my accident.

I padded down the carpeted hallway and found her door slightly ajar. Shadows cast by images from the TV were dancing across the wall. I nudged open the door and saw her sitting on top of the comforter, massaging her legs as she watched *ER.*

"Thanks for knocking," she said, feigning exasperation. "Come on in." She leaned over and turned on the lamp on the nightstand. "Your cousin Imani called. She said to give her a ring sometime tomorrow."

I nodded as I flopped on the edge of the bed. I launched right into the details of my drive home.

"How come when I have one of the best days of my life, something always seems to go wrong? I just ran into the back of a Jeep. Owned by a very handsome brother."

Erika pressed the mute button on the television remote and sat up straighter.

"Maybe it wasn't so bad after all," she said, arching an eyebrow. "What happened?"

As I explained, I noticed her legs. On her fair skin, the bruises looked more terrible tonight than they had yesterday. She saw me and grabbed the sheer bronze robe next to her on the bed. She placed it across her lap and looked at me.

Tears filled her eyes. I knew this wasn't the time to argue with her about how Elliott mistreated her. But I couldn't stop myself from mentioning him.

"Has he apologized yet?" I tried to keep contempt from creeping into my voice.

Erika was so pretty, and she had such a loving spirit. She could be anything she wanted and be with anyone she wanted. More importantly, though, she would do anything to help someone in need or simply because she wanted to make a person feel special. Yet here she was, settling for Elliott, the so-called good catch, because he was handsome and a corporate lawyer. Couldn't she see that she deserved so much better than what he was offering?

I could tell she wasn't in the mood for that lecture—or even Elliott's routine apologies—tonight. When she couldn't hold back the tears any longer, she fell into my arms and shook with sobs.

"Elliott is probably somewhere engrossed in reviewing briefs for an upcoming case, preparing to impress his colleagues and superiors and remind them yet again how wonderful he is," she said resentfully after she had gained some composure.

I wanted to agree, but I knew that wouldn't help her leave him. Tomorrow—no, tonight—even as she drifted to sleep, I knew that Erika would be explaining to herself, as she had often explained to me, why she stayed with him. She'd be convincing herself that no one, including Elliott, could be perfect. It was simply her job to figure out how to keep him happy. Would she realize before it was too late that this so-called job might cost her too much?

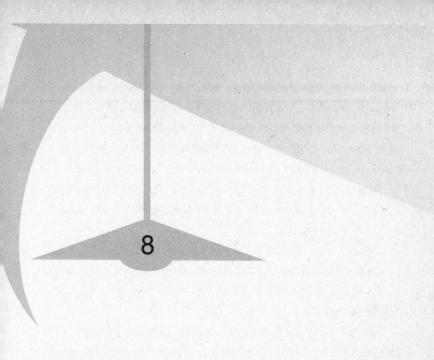

8

While Erika tried to wring the best out of a tired and what I considered dangerous relationship, my favorite cousin, Imani, was basking in the beauty of a powerful love.

Imani didn't question me for calling her at 6:00 a.m. the next day as I drove to the office to get a head start on some projects I'd need to wrap up immediately. I wanted to devote all of my energy to the Aviator Airlines campaign as soon as possible.

Before I could say "Good morning," I heard her shrieking, "I'm getting married! I'm getting married!"

We both laughed. Caller ID had changed America.

"To whom?" I asked with mock curiosity.

If she and John weren't going to tie the knot eventually, I would have given up hope for myself and all of the other single women in the world.

"Hey CeCe," she said, using the childhood nickname

she had given me. She was the only one who had ever used it, which eventually had seemed appropriate. It somehow helped cement our bond. "You know I want you to share this special day with me. Will you be my maid of honor?"

Tears filled my eyes as I pulled into Turner One's parking lot. I used my security pass to enter the private garage before I responded.

"Mani, you didn't even have to ask," I said softly. Then I joked, "You could have just put my name in the program, bought my size eight dress, and told me what time to show up."

Her familiar tinkling laughter filled a place deep within me with regret. It had been so long since I'd heard that—by my own choice.

In dealing with the truth of my parentage, I had struggled with how to interact with the Jasper family. I bore their name, and Herman Jasper was listed as my father on my birth certificate, but now that I knew the truth, I felt counterfeit continuing to mingle with them as family. Did any of them know who my real father was? I hadn't had the courage to tell Imani, let alone anyone else. How would she react?

Instead of chancing it, I had simply made myself scarce. Grad school had kept both of us busy, plus she was involved in a serious relationship with a great guy. That had taken much of her time too.

This morning, though, I wondered whether she had questioned why I had distanced myself.

Does she know the truth about me? I wondered. *And if so, does it matter to her?*

As soon as the thoughts surfaced, so did the answers: *Not enough to leave me out of her wedding. Not enough to push me away.*

Imani was two years older, but she and I had always been close. We were the eldest female first cousins in the Jasper family, and because our mothers had been married to the two younger brothers, the two of them had been close. Even after Herman Jasper's death, Mama and Aunt Jackie remained tight, and Imani and I had practically grown up together.

When she wasn't at my house, I was at hers. She would come to the city for weekend stays at my house, or I'd venture south of the river, into Chesterfield County, for a short visit to the 'burbs. My mother would tease Aunt Jackie each time she'd come to pick me up.

"Don't get my daughter over there in that foreign land, south of James, and forget to bring her back. She'll always be a 'North Sider,'" Mama would say, referring to our neighborhood. She and Imani's mother would cackle like two hens at the corny joke.

Imani was the sister I'd never had, and vice versa. She was close to her older brother, Travis, but there was nothing like the bond between two girls. When we were still in elementary school, long before the days of HIV and AIDS, during one of our Sunday afternoon family gatherings at Gram's we had pricked our forefingers with a safety pin and squished them together so our blood would mix, sealing our bond.

So hearing about her engagement this morning was like finding out that my sister was about to tie the knot. I was so happy for her, for both of them.

Imani and John had met during their undergrad days at Howard University. During their junior year in college, they had both joined a Baptist church near Howard's campus on the same Sunday. Their love seemed to flourish despite their hectic schedules because their faith was the cement for their relationship.

While Imani had gone on to do graduate work in chemistry at Georgetown University, John had remained at Howard to earn an MBA. Now Imani had just landed her dream job as a researcher at the National Institutes of Health in the Washington, D.C., area, and John was completing an MBA Fellows program with the U.S. Department of Labor. He would soon move into a full-time position there.

Imani and John seemed to truly love one another with a Christlike attitude. They both exuded a spirit that attracted others like a magnet, especially young people who wanted to know more about God. They had disagreements like everyone else, but their respect for and devotion to each other was always evident.

Everyone who saw them together saw it. It was the kind of love that I had often prayed for. Unfortunately, John didn't have any available brothers.

But this morning, as I juggled my cell phone with one hand and grabbed the portfolio that held the sketches and memos I had taken home last night with the other, my thoughts weren't on myself. My heart was overflowing with joy for my cousin.

"We're planning to get married in six months," Imani said. "This brother and I are thirty. We've been together for almost ten years, so there's no need for a long engagement!"

We both laughed. But my stomach lurched with her next announcement.

"The wedding is on July 17 at St. Mark's."

St. Mark's. Mama's church. Deacon Gates's church. And, oh yeah, the church Imani had grown up in, just like me. I'd have to return and see Pastor Taylor. Could I handle this?

Imani noticed my silence. "CeCe, you still there?"

I pulled myself back to the present.

"Yep, I'm here," I said. "Just tell me what you want me to do."

"Everything!"

We laughed.

"Seriously, whatever you're able to do, Serena. Gram told me about your promotion, so I know you're going to be very busy. And by the way, congratulations!"

"Thanks," I said.

"Well, since I'm up here in D.C., I'll need some help making arrangements for things to go just right in Richmond. Mom, of course, will have her hands in everything, but I'll need you to serve as my set of local eyes and probably as my referee too!" Imani laughed again. "So Mom may call you to get your opinion on dresses and other things. I'll probably send both of you copies of styles I like."

I have to do this for Imani, I told myself. *I have to.* "Whatever you need me to do, Mani," I said. "I'm here for you. And I'm happy for you. Give John a big old sloppy kiss for me!"

I made sure she still had my cell number and gave her my pager and office numbers so she could reach me whenever she needed me. We hung up as I reached the elevator that would take me to my third-floor office.

I really was happy for her. Those two deserved the best.

See what I can do, if you'll let me lead the way? Love can make everything right.

There was that soft but persistent voice again. Somehow, I knew God wasn't talking to me about romantic love.

The promise I had made to myself last night, just before the accident, came to me. I had said I was going to find another church to call home. I knew I needed to do it soon.

The lights in the corridor automatically came on as I walked down the hall toward my desk. It was so quiet this early in the morning that it was almost eerie.

I reached my workspace, and my eyes zeroed in on the mail I had haphazardly stacked next to my computer the night before. In doing five things at once, I had forgotten to wade through it. This was a sign that today would be crazy busy.

I moved the pile to the corner of the desk before plopping in my chair and turning on the computer. As it booted up, I checked my voice mail, although I didn't expect any new messages this early in the morning. To my surprise, one of my clients, a young entrepreneur who was doing quite well, had called. She had warned me that she slept during the day and worked all night. I scribbled a note on my desk calendar to call her before noon and, as usual, leave a message on her answering machine. I needed to invite her to lunch so I could inform her that someone else at Turner One would soon be working with her company.

Then I turned to my email.

The most recent message had been sent by Max just fifteen minutes earlier. Goodness. Even when I came in before dawn, he managed to beat me to the office.

Serena, FYI, I will announce your promotion in today's staff meeting at 2:00. Todd has asked Mary Grace and Richard to take over your active accounts so you can immediately turn your attention to the airline. Mary Grace and Richard have indicated that they'll be ready to make the transition by the end of the week.

I'm meeting Mr. Takahashi for dinner tonight. Can you join us? It would be good for you two to get acquainted, since he'll make the final decision on whether to accept the campaign we create for Aviator Airlines.

I sat back in my chair and stared at nothing in particular. What had I gotten myself into? Had I bitten off more than I could chew?

"Trust in the LORD with all your heart; and lean not on your own understanding."

That inner voice piped up again, but this time, I felt like the message was coming straight from Mama. She had recited that passage of Scripture to me time and time again over the years as I began making my own decisions and routinely found them challenging or confusing.

"When God is directing you," she'd often tell me, "even when you're nervous you'll be at peace about the place you find yourself in. You'll know that because the situation is in his plan, he'll help you swim safely through the tides."

"Oh, Mama," I whispered to myself as I leaned back farther, molding my frame to the soft leather of the chair, and closed my eyes.

How could the same mother who instilled in me that wisdom have done something so awful? I just couldn't reconcile it.

Maybe you don't have to reconcile it. Just accept it. You're no saint. Neither is she. All have sinned and fallen short.

I sat up and opened my eyes. I shook my head in an attempt to clear my thoughts. I had work to do; I couldn't be distracted by personal issues today. I emailed Max back, confirming that I'd have dinner with Mr. Takahashi and that I would prepare summaries of the accounts I'd been working on to pass on to my colleagues.

As I clicked and sent the email, I began to get excited. I was stumbling in other areas of my life, but not here. At Turner One, I was valued for me, just for being Serena. My hard work was what mattered. My diligence and discipline weren't tied to my parents and their baggage. Here, as long as I helped my company excel, I excelled. The thought was reassuring.

For I so loved the world that I gave my only begotten Son, so that whosoever—so that if you—believe in him, you shall have eternal life . . .

I shook my head again. Had God spoken to me this often when I was faithful? I knew the answer was a resounding yes. When I had regularly studied the Bible and worked with the youths and in other ministries at church, that dialogue with the Lord had become a routine part of my day. It had been a comfortable friendship.

Now when I'd hear that familiar Scripture in my head, I felt like a naughty child. Was he doing that on purpose, or was my guilty conscience causing me to feel this way?

Questions I don't have time to explore right now, I told myself as my phone rang and my day began in earnest.

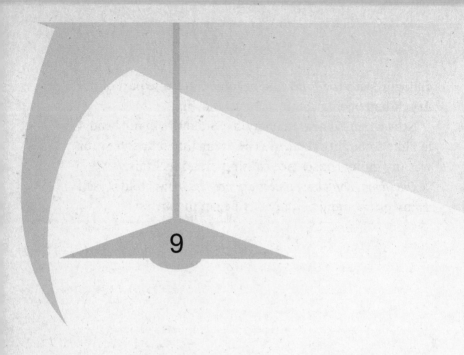

9

If Kirk Franklin could see me now, I thought as I moved my shoulders and hummed "Stomp," the song that we'd worn out in the gospel choir during my latter years at Commonwealth University.

Today, the lyrics were fitting. My promotion had become official, and I was moving into my new office. As I leaned over a large cardboard box and began unpacking the mementos and knickknacks I intended to put on the cherry desk, for some reason I remembered my late-night fender bender a month earlier.

Between preparing for my new tasks at work and keeping in touch with Imani about her impending wedding, the accident hadn't crossed my mind much. The hood of my Camry had a small dent in it, but I'd decided not to risk an increase in my insurance premium by getting it fixed.

The praise and congratulations from most of my co-workers, and the pampering by Vickie, the office assistant

I now shared with another account manager, also had distracted me.

I knew I had moved up the food chain when I arrived at work this morning and found coffee and Danishes next to the tentative agenda for the morning meeting waiting on my desk. I needed to peruse my plans for the Aviator Airlines campaign once more before 10:30.

But now that I had remembered the accident, I wanted to know how my insurance company handled Mr. Mc-Daniels's claim. I glanced at the grandfather clock in the corner of the office and calculated that I had just enough time for a quick call.

I pulled open the bottom desk drawer and rummaged through my purse to find my small address book. Minutes later Kira Smith, my long-time insurance agent, was on the line, explaining that Micah McDaniels had settled the claim at no cost.

"Did I hear you correctly?" I asked. "I know I must have dented the bumper of his Jeep."

"Well, consider yourself lucky, Serena," Kira said. "You must have met a Good Samaritan who didn't want your insurance rates to skyrocket. I called to double-check this while you were holding. It's accurate, and the file will be closed soon. I can send you a letter regarding the outcome if you'd like."

"Please do," I said, with a befuddled frown settling on my face. "Thanks, Kira. I'll talk to you later."

I released the receiver into its black cradle and looked upward. "Thank you, Lord," I said as I folded my arms across my chest.

What was this all about?

I pulled open the desk drawer again and began searching my purse for Micah McDaniels's phone number. I had stuffed the slip of paper with his information in my wallet the night of the accident.

His voice mail picked up after four rings.

"When the call comes, I've got to answer. Unfortunately, you've caught me when I'm working on another request. Leave a message, and I'll respond as quickly as I can. Peace."

I smiled. He sounded just as cool and collected on his voice mail as he had on the night of our brief encounter.

"Hello, Micah, this is Serena Jasper. We met in an unfortunate late-night accident a few weeks ago. I just spoke with my insurance agent, who tells me your claim has been settled at no cost. I'd like to touch base with you and clarify how you were able to repair your Jeep. I hope you don't mind sharing that with me."

I left my work phone number on the voice mail and sat back in my chair again. This was interesting. What had happened?

I tilted my head back and soaked in the warmth of the sunlight that flooded the office through floor-to-ceiling tinted windows. I stared at the top floors of the other downtown buildings within my view and asked myself again how I got here. I shook my head in wonder and glanced at the clock across the room on the wall. It was 9:45 a.m.

The accounts meeting would start soon. I needed to prepare.

After the meeting, I'd be dashing to another engagement. Max had arranged for me to attend a corporate board meeting on his behalf with local United Way officials.

I had planned to meet Tawana for lunch today at Mister P's so we could get reacquainted, but when Max told me he needed me, I had quickly indicated my willingness to go to the luncheon, then cancelled with Tawana despite the disappointment in her voice.

I'll make it up to her, I promised myself. With my newness in this position, I knew I had to prove myself.

The phone rang. I grabbed it quickly.

"Yes, Vickie?"

"A Micah McDaniels is on the line for you."

I gripped the end of the desk and pulled my chair closer. I cleared my throat and tucked a piece of hair behind my ear as if the man could see me through the telephone.

"Put him through."

Seconds later, I heard his striking voice.

"Serena, Micah McDaniels. Nice to hear from you. You have a question about the insurance claim?"

"Yes, Mr. . . . Micah," I said. "I hope you don't mind me asking. I'm grateful that my insurance company didn't have to pay anything, but I'm wondering how you pulled it off."

"Chalk it up to having a buddy who owns an auto repair shop," Micah said.

I could hear the smile in his voice. I remembered the dimples in each cheek.

"He took one look at the car and a few minutes later banged out the dent without much trouble. I wasn't injured—no whiplash to claim, so I thought hey, why not help out a nice young lady who didn't mean any harm?"

Was this guy flirting with me, or was he serious?

"Well, what can I say?" I was grasping for words. "That's so nice of you. Can I take you to lunch?"

"You don't have to do that," he said, more soberly this time. "I'm serious: The dent was really no big deal."

But his kindness was something special, I thought.

"No, I'm serious," I said. "I'd like to treat you to lunch. It's not often that someone does something nice like that. You could've had your friend repair the dent but still have filed the claim so he could be paid."

Micah relented and agreed to meet me later in the week at a downtown café.

"You work down here too?" I asked, after sharing with him that I was an advertising executive.

"Not really downtown, but I get around a little bit of everywhere," he said. "I'll explain more over lunch. See you in a few days. Until then, peace."

I hung up, still amazed by his graciousness. I said another silent prayer of thanks, feeling guilty that I was doing so at my desk, on the run.

I still hadn't kept my promise to find another church, what with the new account. The travel and the meetings required to land this contract left me with little time for getting involved with anything outside the office. That included attending church or regularly participating in a Bible study.

The Bible reading I had planned to do every day as soon as I awoke still hadn't happened. Each morning, as I put it off once again, I made myself feel better by noting that I just didn't have the time to add anything else to my plate.

And while the monthly fee for the Downtown YMCA was still being deducted from my checking account, the eight extra pounds that already had settled on my hips and thighs proved that I hadn't been frequenting the gym as much as I used to.

By the time I wrapped up a thirteen-hour day of planning sessions with the team working on the Aviator Airlines account, I was drained. Renae, a local human resources director I had befriended in step aerobics class, had eventually given up on me. Now, instead of calling to ask when I was going to show up for class, she would send me an email every so often, trying to use advertising lingo to get to me.

"Did you know that just thirty minutes of exercise every day significantly lowers a woman's risk of contracting heart disease and helps her maintain an appropriate body weight?" the message she'd sent just yesterday had read. "Don't be another statistic."

I had quickly typed in a reply: "Yes, I did know. Thanks for reminding me that each day I miss at the gym, I'm closer to doomsday." I had added the smiley face symbol before typing my name.

"Ha ha ha," had been her comeback. "Still want to see you on that workout floor soon, girlie."

I stayed too busy. I arranged weekly meetings with Mr. Takahashi, president of the airline, and his staff to keep them abreast of our progress. Then there were visits to the airline headquarters to talk with employees about the company's values, goals, and morale.

Andrew and Leslie, the assistant account managers Max had assigned to work with me on the campaign, would soon take to the air with me. We planned to board different Aviator Airline flights on the same day, then critique our experiences.

Based on the information we gathered, we'd regroup to brainstorm ideas. Then we'd draft a comprehensive advertising and marketing campaign that included a new company slogan and brand that people would instantly link to Aviator Airlines.

Delta had, among other catchy phrases, "You'll love the way we fly." American Airlines' trademark was "Something special in the air." I was determined that the phrase we devised for Aviator Airlines would be even more memorable.

I was constantly on the go, but I was enjoying the work. Being in charge of pulling together such a significant campaign had my creative juices flowing. In the grocery store, I'd hear part of a mother's conversation with her child and wonder if that would work with the campaign. Or at the cleaners, I'd hear the owner thank a customer with a certain deference and question myself about somehow incorporating that sense of gratitude into the airline's efforts to lure diverse fliers.

I was living, eating, and breathing Aviator Airlines as if I were the CEO of the company. I was having fun. And on top of it, I was getting paid? I laughed out loud at the thought.

You cannot serve two masters . . .

There it came, though. That voice that left me feeling anxious and reminded me how my demanding career meant I was postponing my plans to recommit to God. Once again, I brushed it aside.

Surely God understands, I said to myself as I straightened a stack of folders perched on a corner of my desk. After all, he had granted this gift of my promotion, according to Gram.

Vickie knocked lightly and opened the door.

"The accounts meeting begins in five minutes. And don't forget your United Way luncheon immediately afterward."

I stood and reached for my suit jacket on the coatrack in a nearby corner. I made sure my white silk blouse was properly tucked into my black pants, and I adjusted the jacket on my shoulders. I ran the palm of my hand across my hair to make sure every strand was in place.

"Thanks, Vickie. And can you have the files for my 3:00 p.m. meeting on my desk when I return? I want to glance at them before I meet with Mr. Takahashi about his vision for Aviator Airlines."

She nodded. "Sure thing."

Was that concern I saw in her eyes as I quickly strode toward the door, trying to catch the elevator before it closed? I knew she was thinking about the conversation we'd had a day earlier.

She wasn't timid, that Vickie. As she had tidied my desk, she had questioned how long I would last at the pace I was maintaining.

"Only four weeks into the job and already you're running ragged," she had scolded, sounding a lot like Mama, just a younger and paler version, with auburn hair and lively green eyes. Some office assistants wouldn't dare speak their minds to the ad associates, but Vickie was one of those who felt that if God had placed it on her heart, she better release the knowledge for it to do any good. She had been at Turner One long enough to know that even if she stepped on a few toes, she did her work well enough and spoke enough truth in her tactless assessments that her job was safe.

"Maybe this is just your speed, but I wonder if, sooner or later, you'll decide that this is too much, that you want a life outside of this job," she had told me the day before. "Myra did. That's why she left, you know."

I had given Vickie a curious, "Where did that unsolicited advice come from?" look, and she had quickly turned on her heels and sat down at her desk. She spoke when she wanted, but she also knew when to leave a subject alone.

I hadn't been offended by her comments, but I hadn't forgotten them, either. They seemed to hover over me now as I stepped into the elevator and tried to silence that inner voice that kept repeating the same refrain.

You cannot serve two masters; you hate the one and love the other . . .

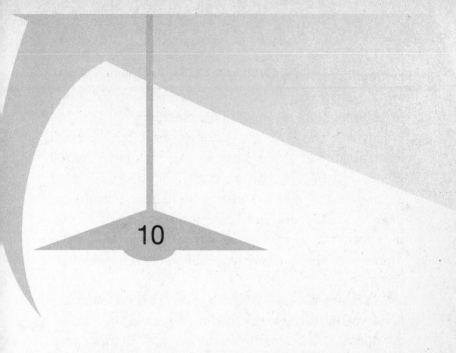

10

I had never been an early riser, but this new Turner One account was turning me into a rooster. In fact, wherever the closest rooster was to Richmond, I had him beat.

I was up and out of my apartment at least two hours before dawn every morning. Most of the time when I returned home, Erika was sleeping. It was almost like not having a roommate, except she kept the kitchen spotless and stacked my mail neatly on the dining-room table each day. If anyone had called, I'd find my messages there too. She was such a mother hen sometimes, and always so thoughtful.

I checked the time on the dashboard's digital clock as I drove toward the office. Tawana probably wouldn't rise to get ready for school for another two hours. If I didn't make this call now, though, I knew it would get put off indefinitely, until I forgot about it again.

Tawana usually kept the family's cordless phone in her

bedroom so it wouldn't disturb Ms. Carson, who came in around dawn after working all night. I knew it would ring three times before going into voice mail.

"Tawana, this is Serena. I know you're probably still in dreamland as I'm leaving this message, but I figured whenever you get it, you'll know that I haven't forgotten about you. I wanted to call and say hi and apologize for having to cancel our lunch last month. If there's another time that you want to try to meet at Mister P's, or even somewhere else, just give me a call on my cell and let me know."

As I hung up and laid the phone on the seat next to me, my thoughts turned to my childhood, growing up without a father and with a mother who struggled to make ends meet. Tawana's existence was somewhat similar.

But Mama had somehow always made sure I had what I needed, as well as many of the things I wanted. I didn't always wear designer outfits, but I was never ashamed to go to school.

In high school, I didn't have my own car like most of my friends or extra money to go to the salon every week to get my hair and nails done. I would have loved to do those things, but I understood our circumstances. Some things couldn't be helped.

Most of my friends loved the Lord like I did too. We were like most other girls our age, into keeping up with the latest trends and looking good, but it wasn't the only thing we were about. Besides, I had reassured myself, my mother was a struggling widow. She was doing the best she could on her salary as a daycare receptionist.

Now that I knew the truth about my father, the thoughts

that had consoled me over the years, that life would have been better, much more comfortable, if Daddy had lived, seemed foolish. I had lost my footing, because those assurances were worthless now. My existence had been crafted around a picture-perfect lie rather than the sordid truth.

I wondered if Deacon Gates had given Mama money over the years to help take care of me. His two sons had driven used but popular model cars in high school. They hadn't gone without.

My chest tightened as the resentment surfaced. I purposely eased my foot off the gas and began to drive more slowly.

I needed to calm down and get this out of my system before I arrived at Turner One. I didn't want any distractions keeping me from focusing on this project.

I took a long, deep breath to center myself.

"God, please help me to move past this," I prayed softly, my eyes open and still on the road. I breathed again.

Hmmph, I realized. *That's the first time in a long time I've sought God's guidance without asking him to make Mama and Deacon Gates feel guilty for their transgressions.*

Today I had asked God to deal with *me*. And as I thought about it, I realized I really meant it. I wanted him to help me move past the pain so I could find some joy again.

I remembered Mama's apology that Christmas when I'd come home from Boston U. She had asked me why I was taking this so hard, why I couldn't forgive her for being human.

Why can't you? What makes you so perfect that you can't let this go?

I didn't feel like probing for answers at the moment. I

thought about Tawana again instead. Spending more time with her would probably help me too. If nothing else, I wanted to let her know that I wasn't going to just brush her off. I was busy, but she still mattered to me.

Five minutes from work, I picked up the phone again and this time dialed home.

Erika would be furious at me for calling so early, but we hadn't talked in weeks. And the short drive to Turner One was my only free time these days.

I could tell that Erika had checked caller ID before answering.

"If you're not calling me because you're dying, you'll be dead before the end of the day," she growled.

"Come on, now! I need to catch up with what's going on with you, Erika. It's a beautiful morning. Rise and shine!" I laughed into the phone, irritating her more.

"If you'd stop spending day and night at Turner One Concepts, we might be able to talk at a decent hour," Erika responded dryly, her voice still thick with sleep. "I bet that's where you're headed now."

I sighed. The Aviator account was a big deal, and this was my first baby. When the new airline campaign hit the market, stories about Turner One and my role in the effort would flood the advertising trade magazines. This multimillion-dollar deal was already big news. So yes, I was headed to work.

"You're the one who said this promotion was great, remember?" I said. "And so far, it is. I'm hoping things will slow down after we get this campaign completed and approved."

Erika was frank as usual. "It won't. It never works that

way. If you do well on this one, you know your boss will hand you the next big-deal contract that comes through the door, and you'll be swamped again. No more dinners at Mister P's any time soon, I guess. But I still love ya."

I didn't respond for a few minutes. Erika was so right. But what could I do? It was the price of success. Didn't Bill Clinton say he survived on only four hours of sleep each night when he was president?

I changed the subject by filling Erika in on my plans to have lunch with Micah later in the day.

"I hope he's not attached," Erika said in an odd voice that let me know she was stretching as she spoke. "You need a date. No, you need a *life*! Speaking of that, Imani called two nights ago. Did you see the message I stuck on the fridge? I didn't leave it on the table with your other stuff because I wanted to make sure you didn't miss it. She has some wedding details she wants to talk to you about as soon as possible."

I hadn't seen the note. When was the last time I had been home early enough to look in the fridge?

"I'll give her a call later today," I said. "God has been so good to her and John."

Erika didn't reply. Still, I prayed for more of these opportunities to talk to her about God, especially since I had begun reading my Bible more often in the past month as a first step to rededicating my life to God. On the mornings I found time to study passages of Scripture, even for just a few minutes, I felt like I was getting to know an old friend again.

I sensed that Erika was watching me closely, trying to figure out what was going on. I had pulled back from God and the church, but now I seemed to be returning to my faith. She was getting mixed messages from me.

For a long time after that truth-telling dinner with Mama, I had followed Erika's lead. I'd sleep late on Sunday mornings and then hit the malls. Or I'd spend the day getting a manicure and pedicure, crash in front of the TV, or hang out with friends.

Each time I thought about my own wishy-washiness, I felt a stab of conscience. What kind of witness was I to Erika? Was I stunting any interest she might have in growing spiritually? I knew, deep inside, that my estrangement from Mama was also hindering my witness to Erika. But I wasn't ready to address that yet.

Besides, I told myself, she had to be ready. She had to desire God. I doubted that growth would happen as long as she dated Elliott.

When they had started seeing each other during our senior year in college, Erika seemed to move farther away from the possibility of a spiritual connection to the Lord. I had fretted about it and talked gently to her about Elliott, but in the end, I decided to give her headstrong ways over to the Lord.

I hadn't let her indecision hamper my relationship with God back then. And even though I was probably confusing her now, I couldn't be silent about my efforts to grow close to God again. I knew from experience that talk of God would inevitably creep into our discussions as my faith grew stronger. It would become such a part of me that I'd mention him subconsciously, as I always had.

Erika used the lull in conversation to make her getaway.

"Since you've been my alarm clock this morning, I guess I'll get off this phone and get started on my day. If I go in a little early, I can leave early to get ready for a dinner party I'm going to with Elliott tonight. Gotta run."

I shook my head. "Bye, girl. Have fun tonight, and call me when you get a chance. You'll know where to find me."

As I pulled into my parking spot at Turner One, I left a message for Imani at her office, urging her to call me at work.

I couldn't wait to talk to her. Right now, though, my work for Aviator Airlines, and within hours, my lunch date with my car accident cutie, beckoned.

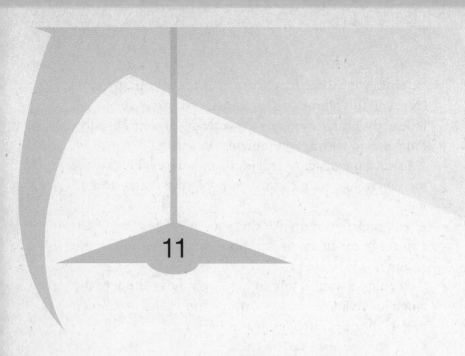

11

By noon I felt like Superwoman, because with half a day still before me, I had already accomplished a dozen tasks.

I ticked them off in my mind as I sat at a cozy table tucked inside a bay window in the restaurant, folding and unfolding the linen napkin on my lap. My seat on an Aviator Airlines flight from Richmond to New York was booked. I had approved the copy for a website logo and slogan and reviewed pictures of models from a variety of ethnic groups and cultures to be used in the print ads.

As I took another sip of water and tried not to stare at the door, I mentally ran through the calls I needed to make when I returned to the office.

Was Micah still coming? I doubted that a man who let me out of a car fiasco would stand me up for lunch.

I glanced at the menu again just to keep busy. When I looked up, a six-foot-two dark chocolate frame stood just inside the door of the café, looking for a face he recognized. I drank another sip of water and waved him over.

When I rose to greet him, he surprised me with a gentle hug.

"Sorry I'm running late," he said in the silky smooth voice I remembered from the night of the accident. "I'm a little behind schedule today."

I self-consciously tucked a piece of hair behind my ear. "Don't worry about it."

I tried not to look too deeply into his dark eyes.

"So what is your schedule? What do you do?" I asked as the waiter left to prepare the Coke with lemon he had requested.

"Serve God," he said and picked up a menu.

"Oh?" I said with a raised eyebrow, remembering the India Arie CD he was listening to on the night of the accident. "How so? Are you in the ministry?"

Micah nodded. His soda arrived, and he took a swig before answering.

"I'm in divinity school full-time at Union University, and I work part-time for an after-school program in one of the local housing projects, mostly tutoring young brothers between eight and twelve years old.

"When I'm not doing that, I stay busy hanging around the church I attend, helping with everything. It's a small congregation, so they need everyone to pitch in to keep things running smoothly."

"Wow," I said, feeling embarrassed about my earlier focus on his physical features. I didn't want to be one of those churchgoing sisters notorious for swooning over ministers. I was certain he got more than his fair share of attention.

"Do you preach?"

"I have on occasion," Micah answered. "But I believe God is calling me to minister to youth, specifically to young black males who lack role models."

I stopped munching on the salad I had ordered with my lunch and looked at him.

"Me too," I said in surprise. "I mean, ministering to young girls. I'm trying to reconnect right now with a teenager I used to mentor several years ago." I hesitated. "I haven't been as committed as I'd like, but I definitely have a heart for youths."

"So we have more in common than a late-night accident, huh?" he said and smiled.

Was I blushing? I couldn't believe this. I quickly changed the subject. "Well, your career path explains your kindness in letting me off the hook with the wreck," I said. "I guess along with thanking you, I should be thanking God."

Micah laughed. It rumbled from deep within and seemed to fill the air with joyful music. For a preacher, he didn't seem to take himself too seriously.

"You could indeed thank God," he said. "But I'll tell you, if there had been some serious damage, I would have pursued the claim. There really was no need to. Besides, I could tell you were on a mission that night."

Before I could respond, our lunch arrived and the conversation dwindled. It was a comfortable silence, as if we had been friends for a long time.

Micah gazed out of the window and admired the view of the James River along with me. We saw men and women in suits sitting on benches eating lunch, as well as older couples taking an early afternoon walk. A few young mothers had bundled up their babies and were pushing them in strollers along the paved sidewalk that bordered the piece of property called Brown's Island.

I didn't have first-date jitters like I had expected. But then again, this really wasn't a date, I reminded myself. Still, I was curious to learn more about Micah.

Before I could launch into another round of questions, he jumped in with his own.

"Tell me about you. What were you up to the night of the accident? Rushing to save someone? The world, maybe?"

Instead of explaining, I teasingly retorted, "What about you? Were you on a ministry call?"

"For myself!" he replied. "I was making a late-night burger run to feed my stomach so I could finish feeding my mind with the information I needed for a test the next morning."

I took a bite of sandwich, hoping that a wilted piece of lettuce wasn't hanging from my bottom lip.

"I was leaving a late dinner with my roommate and heading home, thinking about my plans for a new advertising campaign I'm managing at work."

Micah looked interested. "Sounds like you've got your hands full."

"I do. I work for Turner One Concepts, and the account I've been working on has been keeping me really busy."

"And is your work fufilling?" he asked and cocked his head to one side so he could peer into my eyes.

The question took me by surprise. I stared blankly at

him for a few seconds, taken aback by his forwardness. I wasn't offended, though. I appreciated him for asking. I could tell he was a good listener.

"I suppose," I said. "I've never quite thought about it like that. Sure, I'd like to be able to go to the gym more often, and I've been praying that I'll have enough time to devote to church activities and ministries, but I figure that will all work itself out." I took a sip of water. "This job is great," I continued. "I have my own office, a secretary, and other perks. And I am very well compensated."

I paused. The revelations that were tumbling out almost surprised *me*. Where was all of this soul baring coming from?

"The work keeps me really busy, and sometimes I feel like I don't have a life," I said. "I'm hoping I'll be able to spend some time with the girl I mentioned earlier. I used to work with her at church. And along with finding time to exercise as regularly as I used to, I'd like to leave home after the sun rises and return before it sets. At least some of the time."

I closed my eyes briefly, effortlessly capturing a mental picture of my desires. Micah had asked a question I hadn't really asked myself.

"Sometimes I'd just like to have some quiet time to myself, to do nothing but think boring thoughts or watch Lifetime TV," I said before opening my eyes. "But then I look at where I am and what I'm accomplishing. I'm at the top of my game."

Micah took a bite of the salmon he had ordered and looked out at the river before returning his gaze to my face.

"One of the tough things about life is making choices and not knowing if we're making the right ones," he said matter-of-factly. "You're single with no children of your own, I assume, and no major constraints on your time. So now would seem like the perfect time for you to be 100 percent committed to your job. At least, that's how most of the world sees it."

Micah leaned forward, across the table.

"But what is your spirit calling you to do? In your heart, what would make you the most content right now?"

I stared at him again as I sat there thinking. I parted my lips to answer, but he stopped me by lightly putting his forefinger there. Did he do that with every woman he met for lunch?

"Don't answer now," he said. "Really think about it. Pray about it. Find the answers in your heart. You'll know what they are when they surface. You'll know what you should be doing with your life."

Who *was* this man?

He sat back in his seat and smiled at me. I smiled back and hoped he couldn't hear my heart beating. I decided to play it cool by teasing him again.

"So, do you get all of this wisdom from that secular soulful music you were listening to the night we inconveniently met?"

Again, his laughter filled the air.

"India Arie's music is deep. She's got a positive vibe and she sings about things that matter, not just getting a man and wearing designer clothes. But any wisdom I possess comes from the Word of God. I study the Bible as much as I can so I can try my best to live fully and in

God's will. I mean, even as a man of God, I happen to like good music, including India Arie's." He shrugged. "All I'm saying," he said, returning the focus to me, "is that we often think earning the money, driving the nice car, and having the phat house are the true measures of success. Having those things is fine, but they can't be considered signs of success if they are hindering what God wants us to be doing with our lives.

"That's where studying God's Word and then praying comes in," he continued. "We study to understand how God has operated throughout the centuries and how that might affect our personal situations today. We pray to discern his will and so that we can open our hearts and minds to hearing from him."

Micah caught himself and laughed.

"Am I preaching to you? Sorry. Sometimes I get caught up in what I'm saying, and it just flows."

I laughed too and waved my hand at him.

"Don't worry about it," I said. "Believe me, I'm long overdue for a sermon, Reverend."

Micah was laying some serious stuff on me. I knew I needed to hear it.

How long had I been tuning out those soft whispers to my spirit? Now God was working through one of his foot soldiers.

I felt like I could be honest with this man.

"Micah, it's easy to talk about giving up everything you've worked for, but it's not so easily done," I said. "And why would I want to? I've dreamed for years of being an advertising executive, and here I am, doing it. I'm well respected in my company, I'm leading a major account, and lots of perks come with what I do. I see my promotion as a sign that God can use anybody to do anything as long as they work hard. Am I wrong?"

Micah leaned forward again, this time perching his chin in the palm of his hand and resting his elbow on the table.

"Just follow God's beckoning, and the rest of your path will be revealed to you. I know."

"Oh?" I said. My curiosity was written across my face.

Micah's pager beeped before he could respond. With anyone else, I would have questioned if it were a wife or girlfriend trying to get in touch with him. But this wasn't a date.

He could be attached; I hadn't asked. I felt like he'd let me know if he were. If Micah wasn't for real, then I needed to accept that I'd never find a sincere brother.

He checked the number highlighted on the pager.

"I have to call Pastor Jones back," he said, glancing at his watch. "Look at the time. I didn't mean to keep you more than an hour."

"Don't worry," I said. "I have the flexibility to take long lunches sometimes. But I should be getting back."

I waved for the waiter and paid for lunch as I had promised. Micah insisted on covering the tip.

As we rose to leave, our eyes briefly locked. Not a flirtatious gaze, but a look of blossoming friendship between two souls who had briefly connected. When we stood outside the restaurant preparing to go our separate ways, this time I offered the hug.

"Thank you for your kindness about the car," I said.

He smiled.

"No problem. Next time we get together, let it be on me, and let it be for no other reason but to hang out."

"Deal."

I turned away and began walking uphill, toward my office. A cold wind brushed my face. Before I crossed onto another block, Micah called out to me. He didn't seem self-conscious about others hearing what he had to say, but he strode my way until he stood before me.

He put a hand lightly on my shoulder.

"Think about these words in the book of Jeremiah. Maybe they'll help you figure some things out: 'For I know the thoughts that I think toward you,' says the LORD, 'thoughts of peace and not of evil, to give you a future and a hope. Then you will call upon Me and go and pray to Me, and I will listen to you. And you will seek Me and find Me, when you search for Me with all your heart.'"

Struck by his recitation of the Scripture Deacon Gates had taught me and other members of the Youth Praying Band when I was nine years old, I stood there watching until Micah disappeared around the corner.

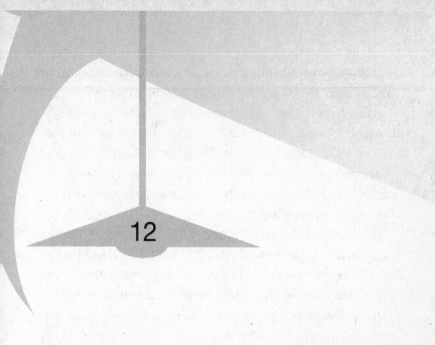

12

Imani was asking a big favor. Despite the wealth of bridal boutiques in the D.C. area, she had found the perfect dress in Richmond.

She and Aunt Jackie had been headed to lunch at their favorite Japanese restaurant on West Broad when they stumbled upon a sale at Mason's Bridal. They went in for a quick look and left with the perfect dress for Imani's perfect day.

Imani had reached me on my cell phone to gush about her find as they were leaving the store. She had wanted me to meet her at her mom's that very night so I could see the dress, but as usual, I was hunkered down at the office.

"I'm breathing, eating, and sleeping an airline these days, Mani," I said apologetically. She understood.

Today her own pressing deadline at work meant Imani was going to miss her first fitting. The seamstress was leaving the country tomorrow for a two-week vacation, but she wanted to have the dress loosely fitted first so her assistants could begin trimming the fabric in some places.

"You're about my height and weight, CeCe," Imani said breathlessly into the phone when I caught up with her at her office. "Please go stand in for me tonight. Tell Ms. Wainwright not to fit it too snugly to your frame, and I promise to come down in the next few days and try it on for one of her assistants."

With her wedding just four months away, she didn't have any time to waste. And she knew I'd do anything for her. But I was going to give her a hard time anyway.

"Yeah, yeah, yeah," I said dryly. "And next weekend John will beg you to stay up there, and you'll have me trying on pumps and wedding veils to see which ones work best. You need a personal assistant."

She laughed.

"I promise not to do that. But I may need you to go by the church and count the number of pews so the florist can gauge how many flowers he'll need. And can you call your mother and ask her to loan me the wedding etiquette and ideas book she's been saving to use for your wedding someday? She said I could borrow it as long as I promise to return it with prayers for your Mr. Right to come along," Imani said and laughed again.

I feigned laughter to hide how unsettled I suddenly felt. Go by St. Mark's? What if Pastor Taylor or Deacon Gates were there? And worse, call Mama?

"Okay, sure," I agreed with as much enthusiasm as I could muster. "I can do those things. When do you need to give the information to the florist?"

"I might be able to do what I need for the florist when

I come down this weekend for my fitting," Imani said. "I told her I'd call by Tuesday. If I don't make it by the church when I'm down there, I'll need your help. You know Mom and Dad are in the Bahamas until next Thursday."

I didn't know, because I hadn't talked to my own mother; I wasn't in the loop on the latest Jasper family happenings. But I didn't want Imani wondering about my ignorance, so I didn't ask her to elaborate on her parents' vacation.

"Anything else, Princess Bride?" I said as I pulled into my parking spot in front of my apartment. I was going to dash in and freshen up before going to try on her special dress.

Wasn't this something? Here I was standing in for a bride, with no ring and wedding on my horizon. *If it were for anyone else but Imani, I might have been mad,* I chuckled to myself.

"I think this is enough of a favor for one day," Imani said. "Thank you, cuz."

"Fuggetaboutit," I joked with her. "See you, girl."

I sat in the car for a few minutes trying to plot my course of action. When was the quietest time to visit St. Mark's? I really didn't want anyone to see me. Why hadn't she asked Mama to count the pews for her? Better yet, why hadn't she called Mama directly to ask her for the wedding book to peruse? Did I have to be the liaison?

I checked myself. This was Imani's wedding. She was extremely busy, and she wanted my help. I would do my best to save my favorite cousin any extra work that I could.

I sighed as I tried to mentally figure out when I could

honor her requests. Since I didn't have a lunch meeting tomorrow, I could for once leave the pile of work on my desk and drive over to St. Mark's to count the pews. If nothing had changed, the doors of the sanctuary would be open on weekdays from 9:00 a.m. to noon so people could come in and pray.

If I can slip into the church just before noon, I might be able to count the pews without being seen by too many people I know, I mused.

And I would figure out how to get the book Imani needed from Mama without having to talk to her. Maybe I could call the house during the day, when I was sure she'd be at work, and leave her a message.

Honor your father and your mother . . .

"What's dishonorable about that?" I questioned aloud. "People leave voice mail messages all the time."

I hadn't talked with Mama since I'd received the promotion. Gram had told her about it, and Mama had sent me a thoughtful card congratulating me. I'd sent her a card back thanking her.

Erika, who had read Mama's card and watched me sit down to sign the one I'd bought in return, didn't restrain her contempt.

"Now, Serena, why are you sending your Mama a card through the mail? If you don't pick up that phone and call her, I'm going to hurt you."

She hadn't raised her hand, of course, but she had stood over me at the kitchen table, leaning on one hip with her lips pursed. She was able to look me in the eye only because I was sitting. In her gray sweat suit and white Nikes, she looked like a fifth-grader preparing for a pep rally. How could I take her seriously?

Maybe that's why she was so feisty, though. She wasn't going to let her size stop her when she meant business.

"You haven't answered me. What is the problem with you and Ms. Jasper? She's the sweetest woman I know. What could she have possibly done to make you act like this?"

I had raised my eyes and looked into her questioning ones.

For a split second, I had considered telling her. But shame coursed through me before I could speak.

What purpose would it serve to put my business and Mama's past out there like that? I trusted Erika, but what if she told her beloved Elliott in a moment of weakness? He disliked me enough that it was the kind of information he'd love to use against me.

Just as the ad campaign for Aviator Airlines hit the market, he'd be at one of his professional bar association socials sharing all the details. Richmond was just small enough for everybody in particular circles to know of everybody else. It wouldn't take long for one of his lawyer friends to have my colleagues in advertising whispering about it.

My silence had let Erika know that I wasn't about to provide answers. She had thrown up her hands in exasperation and walked away. She turned back when she reached the kitchen doorway and got the last bit of frustration off her chest.

"You know, Serena, you've been talking to me for years about God's love and forgiveness and doing unto others as you'd like them to do unto you. Is this how it works?

You harp at me every chance you get about how Elliott is such a dog and how I should leave him alone. Even when you don't say it, I know you're thinking it. Well, look at you. You're dogging your mother. Whatever happened, she's still your mother. You can't just turn your back on her. I guess if I followed your lead, Elliott would be long gone."

My anger had simmered as she said those words that night. She didn't know the real deal about my mother. And how on earth had she twisted my situation with Mama into a reason to stay with her abusive boyfriend?

Pride goes before a fall . . .

I pulled myself out of those memories as I turned the key and entered the apartment. I would need to shower quickly to get to the wedding seamstress's business on time. I would decide later when to call Mama and request the book for Imani.

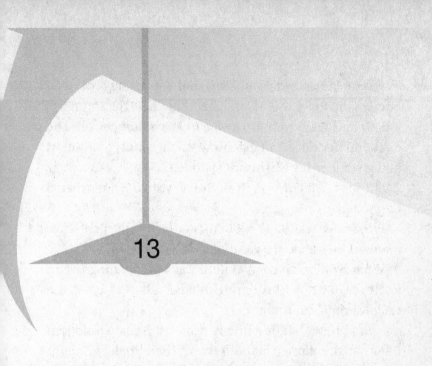

13

I entered the apartment and found Erika in a flurry of activity, hustling to doll herself up and make it to Elliott's company dinner on time. She was nearly in tears.

I measured my words carefully.

"E, are you sure you want to go? Since you know you're going to be late, why not just call Elliott and tell him you came down with a bug? He's going to be upset anyway. So why go and fuel the fire?"

She looked at me and rolled her eyes.

"Serena, I don't have time for one of those you're-better-than-Elliott sermons. And besides, it's not Christlike to lie," she said and looked at me pointedly. "Can you just tell me if the dress works?"

I nodded as remorse filled me. She was right, and I wouldn't have given my advice to lie to Elliott another thought if she hadn't mentioned it.

"You're gorgeous," I said.

She looked stunning in a spaghetti-strap dress of royal purple satin that stopped just above her knee. Her shoulder-length hair was swept up into a modern French roll. The diamond necklace and matching earring studs that Elliott had given her for Christmas sparkled.

She looked picture-perfect. How I wished Elliott treated her better.

Erika ran back to her room to put on her silver stilettos. I paused by the door, wanting to say more.

What would make any difference? I bit my tongue and went on to my bathroom to shower. I had to be at the bridal shop in an hour.

And I knew that despite my protests, Erika would join Elliott at the dinner and afterward spend half the night nursing her wounds again. Just because she had been a little late.

I emerged from my brief shower feeling refreshed. I lathered myself in freesia-scented body lotion, slid into my favorite jeans and sweater, and sauntered into the living room to find Erika just on her way out. Her makeup had been expertly applied, and she was wearing the calf-length black wrap coat Elliott had given her a few birthdays ago. Spring was officially here, but winter hadn't said good-bye yet. It was rather cool tonight, and the coat was chic enough to be appropriate for any season. It was 5:55. The dinner started at 6:00.

She grabbed her purse and snatched her keys from the dining-room table before dashing into the bathroom for a quick once-over in the mirror. After patting her hair, she took a deep breath and gave me a broad smile.

"Bye," she said and waved on her way out the door.

I shook my head and tried not to be exasperated with her.

This is her life. I can't manage it for her. And besides, I cynically told myself, *at least* she *has someone to go to dinner with.*

As soon as I released that thought, I wanted to kick myself. I'd certainly rather be by myself than with somebody who hit me. I looked at my watch before shoving the usually neat Erika's jeans and shirt aside and flopping on the sofa next to the cordless phone. I had to leave in fifteen minutes to make it to the bridal fitting, but I hadn't listened to my voice mail messages all week.

Erika had been so busy with real estate closings that she hadn't been checking the messages either. I wondered if I had missed any important calls. I had.

Tawana had left a message three days earlier. She sounded anxious and said she wanted to talk with me as soon as possible. I wondered why she hadn't called my office or tried me on the cell phone.

Micah had also called. As I listened to his silky voice, I thought about never erasing the message.

"Hi, Serena, how are you? How's that airline project coming? Every time I see a large bird overhead, my thoughts turn to you. I'm calling to see if you want to get together sometime for lunch again, this time on me. Or, if it suits your schedule better, we could catch a movie and have dinner afterward. Give me a ring. Peace."

Was he asking me on a date? Well, all right!

I knew I had no time for leisure—I needed to focus on getting this advertising campaign ready to present to the airline president. But this was worth making time for.

I replayed the message and checked the date and time of the call. He'd left his invitation two days ago.

I sat back on the sofa and closed my eyes. He'd probably think I was playing hard to get. But I wasn't. I just needed to keep up with my life a little better.

I stood and stretched before grabbing my purse and heading for the door.

As I drove toward the bridal shop, I dialed Tawana's number and heard an automated message saying that the phone service had been disconnected.

Her mother must have been late again on the Virginia Power bill. As diligent as Ms. Carson seemed to be, she still struggled to make her ends meet.

When I couldn't reach Tawana, I decided to give Micah a try. A movie was out of the question right now, but I pondered just when I could fit in a lunch date or maybe dinner.

I mean, I *had* to eat. And why not with someone as interesting and handsome as he was?

I soon realized he was quick on his feet too.

"I've been starving, waiting for two days for you to return my call," he quipped when I reached him a few minutes later. "Why don't I meet you somewhere after you finish trying on your—I mean your *cousin's*—wedding dress?"

I laughed. "Now, would I be calling you back about dinner if I were planning my wedding? I don't think so, Reverend. Believe me, my story is legit. And yes, we can meet for dinner tonight, about 8:00 p.m., if that's not too late for you."

"You're talking to a divinity student who usually has at

least three papers due at once, combined with work at the church and serving as an assistant for one of my professors," Micah said. "Eight p.m. is early for me."

We agreed to meet at an Italian restaurant not too far from the bridal shop. I was excited and a little nervous.

What would we talk about this time?

Turns out, everything.

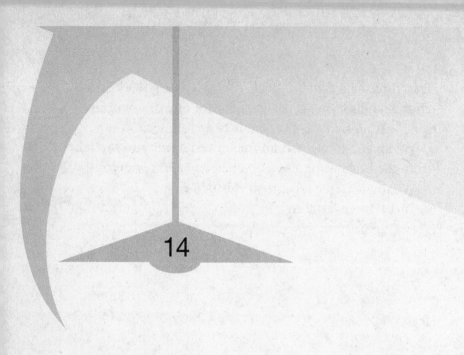

14

Micah appeared to be a serious, taking-care-of-business kind of man, but he was also hilarious.

He had me in stitches, explaining how he'd grown up in a small Oklahoma town where cows were as frequent on the roads as cars. Surprisingly, though, he had the nerve to call the Southern gentility and old-school traditions of Richmond stuffy.

"If your mama's grandmama's mama wasn't born and raised in Richmond, you really aren't a native," he said in mock horror. "My pastor has lived here for twenty-five years, but he's still considered a newcomer."

I laughed as I nibbled at my fettuccini primavera. The dimmed overhead lighting and candles flickering on the tables set a nice mood. There were only five other diners scattered throughout the restaurant, so it almost seemed as if we had the place to ourselves. I was so glad I hadn't put on my favorite well-worn sweats before checking my messages and calling him back.

"I hear that's true about Richmond," I said, not willing to admit that I'd been told more than once how the city I was born and raised in could be somewhat cliquish and hard for outsiders to comfortably settle in. "But it sounds like you're here to stay," I said, referring to our earlier talk about his plans to launch a father-son community-wide ministry when he graduated from divinity school in another year.

He shrugged and swallowed another forkful of lasagna.

"I suppose so," he said. "This would be a logical place to get the ministry off the ground since I have the support of my pastor and my professors. They know a lot of people in the community. But then, who said God was logical? If I worked from logic, I wouldn't be here in the first place."

I waited expectantly for him to continue.

"This story is getting more interesting with each bite," I said.

He flashed that one-hundred-watt smile and laughed at my curiosity. I didn't waver; he was the one who brought the subject up, so now I wanted to know.

"Well, I might eventually obtain a doctorate in theology, but my parents are still struggling with the fact that I've given up being Micah McDaniels, M.D."

He lowered his head and took another bite. Then he turned those deep brown eyes toward me, waiting for my response. I gave him a wry smile, thinking he was joking. He could tell I didn't believe him.

He pulled out his wallet and removed an ID card, which he slid across the table.

Oh.

It bore a thinner, wearier-looking image of him and had the words Bellevue Hospital, New York University School of Medicine, emblazoned across the top.

"This isn't a joke?" I finally asked.

"Remember that Scripture from Jeremiah I quoted you a few weeks ago, about God knowing the plans he has for us and his ability to speak to us if we're willing to seek him?" Micah said. "I finally had to stop going my own way and start traveling the path God desired for me."

I held the ID card in my hands and stared at him. This man was something else.

"Sounds crazy, I know," he said. "My parents asked if I were going through some sort of identity crisis, or if I feared success." He laughed. "You just don't know how many theories abounded. But the simple truth was, God wouldn't leave me alone. He kept pestering me until I yielded.

"The thing is, God had never told me to go to medical school. That was my father's dream. Pop never got the chance because he had to go to Vietnam, and when he returned, my mother got pregnant right away. He had to take a job at the local paper mill to support the family.

"From the time I was about ten, my father talked about his firstborn going on to be a doctor. I was good in science, I liked the idea of having an important career, and I figured I could help some people along the way too. So I went for it."

Micah rested his elbows on the table and continued.

"I went to Xavier University in New Orleans for undergrad and to medical school at Temple. All along, I kept hearing the Lord. 'Man can repair the body, with my help, but you are called to be a healer of souls, Micah. You are chosen to heal the land.'"

He glanced at me to see if I was taking this all in, taking him seriously. I was.

"Doctors heal, right? Surgeons heal. I was going to be one of the best surgeons in the country. When I got the residency in New York, I knew I was on my way. I was working with some of the best doctors in the country. God was blessing me, I thought.

"But you know what? The day I started that residency, I stopped feeling right with myself. I didn't feel at peace, didn't feel like I was on the right path. I couldn't sleep—and not just because of the long hours. When I was able to shut my eyes, my dreams were weird, my thoughts were restless. I found myself praying less and meditating less, and working harder to make myself feel better."

Micah laughed softly.

"Funny thing was, the more I left God out of my life, the harder things got. I had somewhat enjoyed the medical training up to that point. But when I went in to see patients, I found myself talking to them about issues other than their physical ailments. I wanted to pray with some of them so badly. I wanted to tell them about the God who loved them unconditionally, the God who was longing to give them the peace and strength they desired, as well as health for their bodies.

"But I couldn't. We were instructed throughout med school not to sway patients with our personal beliefs, religious or otherwise. I mean, a few times, I stepped over the line and shared my faith. I recommended one woman whose mother had Alzheimer's to a local church for prayer and support. I advised a stressed-out young mother whose son had chronic asthma to read the book of James for solace. But I wanted to do so much more. I wanted to be their lifeline to the Lord."

Micah paused, caught up in his memories. I sat silent, waiting.

"And finally, I knew. After months of not reading my Bible, I woke up one night from another jittery sleep and opened it. I turned the pages until I felt compelled to stop.

"There in Luke chapter 14 was my answer. Jesus told the people who followed him as he preached that if they really wanted to serve him, they had to forsake all that they had: 'If any man come to me, and hate not his father, and mother, and wife, and children, and brethren, and sisters, yea, and his own life also, he cannot be my disciple.'"

Micah's eyes were glistening.

"I knew then. I knew that although God could use me to heal people with my hands and my surgical skills, he wanted me to heal them with his Word. I had to obey.

"A year later, after I resigned from the residency and applied to several divinity schools, I found myself here in Richmond, at Union, preparing myself to do what God intended all along."

I shook my head in wonder. A few minutes passed before I spoke. When I did, the questions flowed.

"Do you know what kind of courage that took? What did your parents say? How did you know that it was really

God speaking to you? And couldn't you have been both a doctor and a minister?"

I was asking about his situation, but in the back of my mind, I knew I was seeking answers for my own circumstances.

"Like I said, my folks thought I had gone stone crazy. And why shouldn't they? I had devoted all these years to achieving this goal, and then I just quit.

"But courage really wasn't part of the process. I wasn't scared, because I knew I was doing what God wanted me to do," Micah said. "He had been trying to tell me for years, and I had brushed his beckoning aside. I tried to do things my own way. He didn't ask me to go to medical school; that was my doing.

"And if I had had a passion for medicine, or even felt compelled to serve people in that way, I know I could have combined medicine with the ministry. But it was such a struggle that I knew trying to maintain the medical profession would pull me farther away from God's plans for my life.

"When I finally sat up and heard God clearly, I was filled with peace. I knew that everything I was about to give up would be worth it if I pleased God. I haven't had a sleepless night since then," he said.

"I'm still paying back my student loans from medical school, but I gratefully write those checks. If I hadn't gone through that period of trying to do my own will, live life my own way, I doubt I'd be as close to God as I am now. I doubt I'd be living such a divinely directed life.

"That bill every month is a regular reminder of how blessed I am and how thankful I ought to be that I finally sat up and took notice of God's purpose for me. I just feel honored that he wants to use me in this way. And thankfully, my mother finally came around. She understands that I'm following the Bible she raised me to live by." Micah smiled ruefully. "I'm still working on Pop."

I squeezed his hand.

"Praise God for you, Micah. I'm listening for his direction in my life now."

He smiled but didn't ask me to elaborate.

"He's just waiting on you to be ready to hear him, Serena. When your heart is open to him, when you're focused on him, you will hear clearly what God wants you to do. Believe it."

Before I could respond, our waitress approached.

"Any dessert tonight? Want to share a piece of cake or another delicacy?"

We both declined, and she pulled our check from the pocket of her shirt.

"If you don't mind, I'll give you your ticket now and leave you in my co-worker's hands. They need my help at the bar for the rest of the evening."

Micah gave the woman her tip and took the bill.

"This one's on me," he said.

I shrugged. "I'm not going to argue with you."

We made small talk as we waited for the new waitress to come by and pick up his debit card.

"Is it okay if I call you Reverend Doctor McDaniels?" I teased.

"Watch it," he warned me and feigned a frown. He said he often talked with youths about his decision, but he wasn't big on using fancy titles.

"A lot of the time they separate people. If someone has to call me Reverend instead of Micah, they feel like I'm the school principal instead of their friend."

Micah looked up and smiled. Our new waitress had appeared and was standing just behind my seat.

I turned and looked into the girl's face. My heart almost stopped. It was Tawana.

"T!" I said as I rose to give her a hug. "What are you doing here? The last time we talked, weren't you still working at Mister P's? And I got your message tonight—the one you left a few days ago. I'm sorry I didn't get back to you sooner."

I wouldn't embarrass her in front of Micah by explaining that I'd tried to call and couldn't get through.

Tawana, looking a little unsettled, nodded. Her hair was pulled back into a disheveled ponytail, and her shirt poked out of one side of the waistband of her black pants.

"That's okay," she said in a way that let me know it really wasn't. "I was calling to get your advice about whether to leave Mister P's and take this job. But when I couldn't get you, I went ahead and took it. They pay more here. This is my second day."

I wanted to question the longer hours, which would interfere with her studies, but I didn't. I had missed my opportunity to have a say when I hadn't returned her call.

"Is everything else going okay for you?" I asked.

"Not really," she said flatly. She glanced at Micah. Her eyes indicated that if he weren't there, she'd say more.

"Call me tomorrow on my cell phone," I said. I gave her another card with the number, in case she had lost the last one. She tucked it in her shirt pocket.

"I'll call you tomorrow," she said.

And finally, I introduced her to Micah.

"This is my friend Tawana," I told him. I turned back to Tawana. "How are things with your mother? Getting along better?"

She shrugged. "It's been a long time since you and I have talked. Some things never change, and then again, everything does."

She looked at Micah again and seemed to decide his presence didn't matter. "I called you the other day to talk to you about this job and something else too. I found out three weeks ago that I'm pregnant. I'll start showing before long, and I wanted to ask you if I should tell the manager here who offered me the job. I decided not to, but now I'm wondering if she'll fire me when she finds out."

Micah lowered his head to give me privacy with Tawana in this moment.

I was stunned. Obviously, this girl still needed someone to talk to. Obviously, she still needed me.

When I had left St. Mark's, I had left behind more than Deacon Gates and Violet Jasper. I had no one to blame for that but myself.

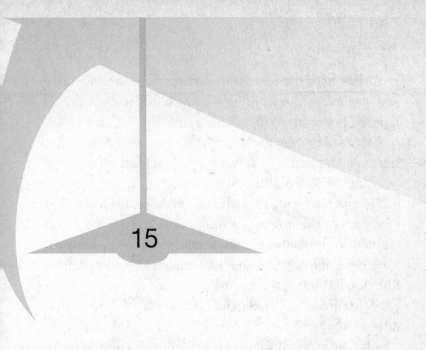

15

I wept on the drive home as I thought about Tawana's predicament.

Lord, forgive me for my selfishness, I prayed silently as I drove. *I was so caught up in my own pain and in getting back at the people that I thought were hurting me that I never stopped to consider the people I was hurting.*

I had left behind Tawana and a couple of other girls who had depended on seeing me weekly and calling me for advice whenever they needed it. All I had become to them was another casualty; someone else who had entered their lives for her own purposes and then disappeared without uttering good-bye. Now here was Tawana, pregnant and obviously scared.

After her revelation, Micah had excused himself to give us a few minutes alone. Tawana couldn't talk long because she had other tables to serve, but she quickly informed me that her twenty-one-year-old boyfriend had stopped returning her calls when she told him the news. When he saw her in the neighborhood now, he turned away and ignored her attempts to talk to him.

Her mother was furious and was threatening to put her out. She had told Tawana she wouldn't be working overtime to feed another person.

Tawana was trying to hold her own. She and I had talked many times about her dreams of becoming a lawyer. She wanted to prosecute criminals and try to keep drugs off the streets of neighborhoods like the one she called home. She worked hard to get good grades so she could win a college scholarship. That would be the only way she could afford to go.

Now she was struggling to keep her grades up and make it through the end of the school year. The baby wasn't due until September, and she was still experiencing morning sickness.

I squeezed her hand and stood to hug her again, but she backed away, conscious of the other diners.

"Oh, Tawana," I said softly.

I wanted to beg her forgiveness for abandoning her, but I knew from experience that Tawana had heard enough empty apologies. Instead, I resolved to recommit myself to helping this girl.

"I know it's been a long time since we were friends," I said, "but I'm still here for you. I left you hanging before, but I want to do whatever I can to help you now."

She gave me the obligatory smile. She promised to call me, then she moved on to the next table of customers. I knew, though, the responsibility lay with me.

It was up to me to keep in touch at this point, to prove

that I really intended to be there for her. She was sixteen and needed all the help she could get.

Micah hadn't asked questions when he walked me to my car, but I was certain he could tell I was upset by Tawana's revelation. Before opening my door for me, he turned and grasped my shoulder.

"Don't beat yourself up over this," he said. "We're all human—you're human. Sometimes we get so wrapped up in our personal dramas that we don't really have enough to offer anyone else. I'm not saying that's a good excuse, but it's reality.

"When you were away from her, you were probably handling all you could," he said. "For some reason, God has brought you two together again. Just go with that and don't keep dwelling on the past."

We hugged before getting into our cars and driving off at the same time.

Despite Micah's reassurances, I couldn't keep the guilt from surging or hold the tears at bay.

Here I was, thriving at work, and Tawana, who I knew had the same kind of potential, was about to be arrested in adolescence. Would this baby keep her from graduating? Would she spend the rest of her life in the crime-ridden, desolate neighborhood she was growing up in, struggling like her mother to earn a decent living?

Before I finished asking myself those questions, I knew the answers. I was going to have to make sure those things didn't happen. Tawana needed me now. Was I up to the challenge?

With me, all things are possible.

The tears stopped as I pulled into the parking lot of

my apartment complex. Intellectually, I knew this. Deep within, did I really believe it?

Too wound up to go to sleep, I spent the next hour curled up on the sofa, staring blankly at a room makeover on TLC. As the show unfolded and was interrupted by commercials, images kept running through my mind of the many times I had called Tawana to cancel a visit or reschedule something we had planned to do together. I recalled how patient and forgiving she had been.

Now it's too late, I told myself.

When an Aviator Airlines deadline or other pressing emergency had left me unable to be there for her, Tawana had filled those lonely hours by seeking attention in the wrong place. She was a shy girl who usually stayed inside her family's apartment instead of roaming the neighborhood with other girls her age. She was polite to the local drug dealers, some of whom were her former classmates, but she stayed out of their way as much as she could.

She had an A average that she wanted desperately to maintain. Her mother had been telling her for years it would be her ticket to a better life.

Tawana had been teased by some of the other neighborhood children for being so quiet and always keeping her head in a book. In the past, it had never seemed to bother her. She knew she was on a mission.

Now I wondered when that had changed. What had led her to join those kids on the stoop, where older boys and young men looked for fresh prey? How had she succumbed to the lines of suave-talking Antonio, when before she had always seemed to know better? She had given me her one-time boyfriend's name and age, but nothing more.

Maybe she gave up hope. Maybe she decided to accept love, or what masqueraded as love, because nothing else was readily available.

I hugged the paisley sofa pillow as my guilt continued to surge. A fresh wave of tears was coming when I heard Erika's key in the door.

I sat up and waited for her. She wouldn't believe it when I told her Tawana was pregnant.

She entered slowly and closed the door behind her. That was unusual; Elliott usually escorted her in after one of their dates. She turned toward me, and I gasped.

What had happened to the doll who left home four hours ago? Her hair was tousled, mascara was running down both cheeks, and her bottom lip was split and swollen.

I jumped up from the sofa and grabbed her forearms. Shame and hurt pooled in her eyes. She hadn't wanted me to see her this way.

"I don't know why he gets so angry," she said in a little-girl whisper. "I was only twenty minutes late for the dinner. No one had even ordered."

"That no good . . ."

I prayed for God to keep the foul words racing through my mind from leaving my lips. I led Erika to the sofa and sat next to her.

"Erika, why . . . ?"

My question trailed off. I knew there was no legitimate explanation for the way she looked, the way she had been treated.

"I'll get some ice." I dashed to the kitchen and filled a plastic zipper storage bag with ice. I wrapped a dishcloth around the bag and walked back to the sofa.

Erika was sitting there, her arms wrapped around herself, rocking. She stared off into space. I sat beside her again and held the ice to her lip. She laid her head on my shoulder and sobbed.

On TV, two sets of neighbors were viewing the rooms they had decorated for each other on *Trading Spaces*. A brunette and her bald, bespectacled husband were shrieking over their transformed family room.

The sound of their laughter mingled with Erika's cries. I felt sick. I picked up the remote and turned off the TV.

I put the ice back to her lip and stroked her hair. Her head still rested on my shoulder.

"I know he loves me," she said between her whimpers. "I just know he does. Next time I'll be on time."

I knew then not to bother suggesting that we call the police. All I could do was pray.

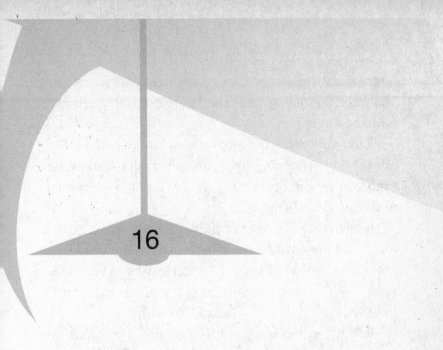

16

Just as the sun appeared, I rose from my knees and sat on the edge of the bed. It had been a long time since I'd knelt and talked to God. But after last night, I knew where I had to turn.

I had not felt God's presence as I prayed for Tawana and Erika this morning, but I knew he was there. The lack of connection was my fault. It was like calling up a relative I hadn't seen in years and trying to pick up where we left off. There were going to be some awkward moments.

Still, I believed God heard me. I trusted that he would answer my plea for his miracle-working power to touch my friends. Right now, though, I wished he'd give Erika a burning bush experience like Moses's. She had to stop letting Elliott abuse her.

I knew that first she had to acknowledge that she was being mistreated. Elliott would send a bouquet of flowers today, as usual, with a card saying he was sorry and he hoped she was feeling better. As always, Erika would melt and forgive him. Couldn't she figure out how to forgive him *and* forget him?

I had a mountain of work waiting for me at the office, but I was considering staying home part of the morning. I thought I should be here in case he decided to come by to pick another fight.

Then I remembered the prayer I had just uttered. I thought about what Mama would tell me: "You've already prayed, Serena, so give it to God and leave it in his hands. The more you keep hanging on to the problem, trying to solve it yourself, the less God can do with it."

Even when I didn't want to, I had to admit that my mother was right. I sat on the bed for a few more minutes before walking down the hall to Erika's room.

I tapped lightly on the door and heard her tell me to come in. She was lying on her side in bed, facing away from the door, when I entered.

"Guess I won't be showing houses today," she said dully. "Can't explain away this golf-ball-sized lip."

I sat on the bed and waited. She didn't turn toward me.

"You want anything? Does it still hurt? I can stay with you today if you want."

Erika shook her head. "No, I just want to be by myself, if you don't mind. Take the phone off the hook. I don't want to hear from him today."

I picked up on the word *today*. She hadn't said *ever again*.

I thought I'd try.

126

"Erika, do you want to report him? He'll keep doing this as long as he knows he can get away with it."

She still didn't look my way.

"No, Serena. Please just stay out of it. I'll be fine. I just need to be alone. Thanks for your help, but please go. I'll see you later."

I could tell she was upset. I didn't want to force myself on her. I stood up and walked toward the door.

"See you tonight, Erika," I said softly before closing her door behind me.

I leaned against the wall outside her bedroom and closed my eyes. I had failed to help Tawana. Should I stand by and watch Erika suffer too? Wasn't there something I could do?

I knew I needed to get to work, but right now, I just couldn't focus. I picked up the cordless phone off the stand in the hall and dialed Vickie's number.

"Good morning," I said when she answered. Vickie always teased me about being so perky in the mornings that I could take over Katie Couric's job. I tried to sound like my usual cheerful self.

"Is it a good morning?" she asked. "My clock says it's 8:00 a.m., and you aren't here. Has someone superglued you to your bed?"

It felt good to laugh.

"I'm just taking a creative break. I'll be in sometime after lunch."

Vickie couldn't let this opportunity slide. "I just can't believe it. Serena Jasper is actually taking some time for herself. She's coming to work after the sun has risen,"

Vickie laughed. "See you this afternoon, Miss Lady. Enjoy your morning."

I ended the call and headed for my shower. Before 10:00, I had put on my navy-and-white jumper set and sneakers and hopped in my car. Erika had asked for space, and I wanted to give it to her.

It was a beautiful day for a walk. Late April, sunny and cool. I pulled into the parking lot at Maymont Park just as a busload of preschool students were unloading to visit the animals in the small Children's Farm.

I walked down the path, past the horses and cows, and took a seat on a bench near the Japanese Garden. The silence and beauty of the foliage enveloped me. I needed this respite from the office and the drama that filled the rest of my life.

My thoughts turned to the night before. In the span of a few hours, I had gone from trying on my cousin's wedding dress and having dinner with a handsome friend to finding out that a girl I had once mentored was pregnant and that my roommate had been beaten up again.

I threw my head back to clear my thoughts. This setting was too lovely to dwell on the ugly.

I focused on Micah and all that he had shared with me over dinner. What a powerful testimony.

His relationship with God had to be deep for him to take such a drastic leap of faith. Instead of listening to the people around him, the people he cared about most, he had brazenly followed his calling.

Sitting there thinking about it, I wondered if God was asking me to make some drastic changes. I knew I wasn't praying and worshiping as I should. Were there other areas I needed to perfect as well?

After our conversation last night, I knew what Micah would say: Don't compare my situation to his. Talk to God myself. Listen to hear what he's telling *me* to do.

I had tried that this morning when I knelt in prayer. I was going to have to stop making idle promises and surrender to God.

I stood and walked farther along the winding path until I reached a hilly slope of the park. A man sat on his jacket spread on the grass and strummed his guitar. There was an empty bench nearby where I could enjoy his music without invading his space.

I sat and took in my surroundings. No one but God could create this lush green grass that smelled so sweet, or the beautiful roses, tulips, and azaleas that splashed color across the landscape. I loved spring.

The sound of young kids drew my gaze to a nearby spot. Two scrawny children, a boy and a girl, sat on a rumpled blanket and extended their hands to the young woman with them, pleading for something.

"Wait a minute!" she said in exasperation. "Settle down, Damon, Mia. This is all Mommy has right now. I'm going to split it in two, and you each can have a half, okay? Give me a minute."

The children quieted down and watched as their mother tore something in half. She placed the halves on napkins and handed them to her children.

Sometimes I could be so nosy. I leaned forward to get a better look. It was a peanut butter and jelly sandwich. Just the one for two children.

My heart sank.

Nearby, a hot dog vendor had set up shop and was whipping out all-beef wieners to adults and children who had come to the park for an early lunchtime break. Before I could talk myself out of it, I fell into line and ordered four.

I struggled not to drop the food as I approached the lady and her children. The kids were just finishing their halves of the sandwich and looking expectantly for more.

"Hi," I said, standing there with my offerings. The aroma of the hot dogs floated on the air. "Mind if I sit here with you guys? I just happen to have some extra hot dogs. I can't eat them all."

The woman looked at me suspiciously. Shame clouded her face. She was preparing to refuse when her children ran to me and jumped up and down.

"Mommy! Mommy!" they yelled. "The lady's giving us hot dogs. She's got food for us!"

The young mother pressed her lips together and bowed her head to hide her embarrassment. I could see she was struggling. I understood. Who would want a stranger to have to feed her children? But how could she say no?

She made a space for me on the blanket and motioned for me to sit down.

"I'm Serena," I said.

"Monica," was her soft reply. She motioned toward her son and daughter. "Damon and Mia."

I asked the children whether they wanted mustard or ketchup or both on their hot dogs. Monica finally raised her eyes when I held one out to her.

"Mothers have to eat too," I said.

She took the food and smiled.

"Thank you," she said softly, in heavily accented English. "You didn't have to do this, but God bless you."

"God has already blessed me," I said. "He's allowing me to have lunch with you."

She slowly let down her guard as we ate.

"We live in River Court, in the north side," Monica said about the subsidized housing complex that I used to pass on the way to my mother's house.

"My husband is a painter and handyman. He works for a local builder, doing odd jobs. When the weather is bad, he can't work. On good days, he works long, long hours to take care of us."

I nodded, letting her know I understood that despite her husband's diligence, the pay was not always enough to meet their needs.

"I had a job serving food at a downtown café, but I got laid off when business slowed down," she said and shrugged. "Andre—that's my husband—said I should just stay home with the kids for now so we wouldn't have to worry about paying for day care."

She turned her head toward Damon and Mia, who were rolling in the grass nearby and giggling.

"I try to stay out of that cramped apartment as much as I can, and it's too dangerous to let them play outside over there. Whenever I have an extra couple of dollars, I take the bus or beg a neighbor with a car to bring us here.

"I love this park," Monica said wistfully. "It's so pretty. It takes my mind off that ugly place where I'm raising my kids."

I understood.

"You can sit here for hours and just enjoy its beauty," I said, before changing the subject back to River Court.

"I'm familiar with the housing complex where you live. I have a friend who lives there with her mother," I said, thinking of Tawana. This young mother's plight saddened me because I could see how Tawana might face a similar fate.

Monica said she was nineteen. She had run away from home in New York three years earlier to follow her boyfriend, now her husband, Andre. They still were together, but with money so tight, things weren't the greatest between them right now.

I was surprised she told me so much, but I could tell she trusted me. I had felt the same when I met Micah.

It was obvious that Monica, like Tawana, needed a friend. She needed some help with tapping into area resources that could make life easier for her and her family.

I knew I couldn't become a long-term friend—look how I had neglected Tawana. But there was the perfect agency not too far from where she lived . . .

Finally, I remembered the name. Hope House.

I had volunteered at the agency for struggling low-income families every year I attended Commonwealth University. Located in the city's Oregon Hill section, Hope House had been near enough to campus for me to go by frequently. I had helped with everything from tutoring elementary students and planning activities for senior citizens to helping a single mother plan a budget.

It had been such gratifying work. And I knew it was making a difference.

"I hear your slight accent, but you say you're from New York. Are you a U.S. citizen?" I asked.

Monica nodded.

"My family immigrated from Puerto Rico when I was five, and we all have our citizenship now. But I grew up in a household where my mother and grandmother continued to speak their native language, and in a neighborhood with the same influence. So I haven't lost my accent yet."

She said her husband was African-American and also from New York.

"He's a hard worker; he's just having a tough time," she said.

I explained that I had asked about her citizenship because I wanted to refer her to a nonprofit agency for families that would ask similar questions before attempting to help her find work or go to school.

"I don't have a phone right now," Monica said. "Can I give you my address?"

I jogged to my car and retrieved my purse. I jotted down her name and address and wrote "Hope House" on a slip of paper for her. I gave her enough change to call the agency from a pay phone.

"It's on the bus line," I assured her.

The children, their bellies now full, had gone off to play nearby. Monica's countenance had changed. She cheerfully called out to them to come and say thank you and good-bye to me.

"I'm going to call this place as soon as I get to a phone," she promised as she folded her blanket.

I stood and helped her.

"You know what? I have my cell phone on me. Let's call now."

My experience with Tawana had shown me it was best to act sooner rather than later. I called information and asked for Hope House's number.

When I dialed it, a familiar voice answered. I couldn't place it, but I assumed it was a staff member who had worked there years ago when I volunteered on a regular basis.

"This is Serena Jasper. I'm a former Hope House volunteer, and I'm calling to put a young family that lives in the River Court community in touch with your organization. The husband works, but I think they can benefit from the services you offer."

"Well, my goodness," was the response from the other end. I held the cell phone away from my ear and looked at it. Had I dialed the right number?

"Is this Hope House?" I asked.

The woman on the phone chuckled.

"It certainly is, Serena. I'm just surprised to hear from you. This is Callie, your former neighbor at West End Forest apartments. Remember me?"

I thought back to the years I had lived off Glenside Drive before going to BU. Callie. The neighbor I had hugged when I received my acceptance letter for grad school. Wasn't she a teacher?

"Callie, I do remember you," I said. "How are you?"

If voices could paint pictures, I knew she was beaming.

"Serena, I've waited so long for this moment. I didn't know where you went after leaving for Boston, and I've wanted to track you down for at least two years."

Monica stood there expectantly, waiting to see if this agency could help her. I was puzzled.

Callie continued. "Serena, sometimes you just don't know whom you're touching when you do positive things. The year you left for Boston, I began to do some serious soul-searching about my life. I stopped stuffing my feelings down with food and prayed for God to tell me how he wanted to use me.

"I've always had a heart for working with children, of course, but I wanted to do something other than teach. Last year I completed my master's degree in social work at Commonwealth University. I'm the assistant program director here at Hope House.

"So thank you. I know God used my encounter with you that day you received your acceptance letter to Boston University to motivate me. I realized that even at my age, I could make a difference. And lose that extra fifty pounds that was weighing me down!"

She laughed heartily and waited for my reply.

The whole spiel left me stunned.

"Callie, I don't know what to say," I said. "That is so wonderful. Sounds like you've done all the hard work, so please don't give me the credit!"

I laughed, but I really was touched. She and I chatted for a few more minutes, and I passed the phone to Monica so Callie could get her information and follow up with her.

As Callie and Monica talked, I got down on my knees and embraced Damon and Mia. They tackled me with hugs. I picked myself up just as Monica was ending the call.

"She says they have activities there for the children too," Monica said. Her excitement was evident in the way the words poured from her lips. "She says they can help our family in lots of ways."

I made a mental note to call back and ask about services for Tawana too.

Monica stood there, as if embarrassed about how to leave. I smiled. She said thank you with her eyes.

"Thank *you*," I said aloud. "It was so nice to meet you. You and these little angels have helped make my day."

The surprise reconnection with Callie had been the icing on the cake. God got an A-plus for creativity when it came to getting his message across to me.

17

The light tap on the door startled me. I slowly raised my head from the desk and rubbed my neck, struggling to remember where I was.

Of course. At the office. At my desk.

"Come in," I said softly.

Vickie entered carrying a cup of coffee and a plate of pastries.

"Tell me you didn't sleep here last night."

I sat up and tried to get my bearings. "I don't know. What time is it?"

"Eight-thirty Monday morning. You *did* sleep here, didn't you?"

I looked at her sheepishly.

"I worked through the night. Couldn't help it. But I've got a change of clothes here. Let me eat a doughnut and get a cup of coffee in me. I'll go down to the basement and shower and change. What time is the meeting?"

Vickie shook her head in disapproval at the fact that I'd come in on Sunday and stayed through the night. "Your meeting with Max and the Aviator Airlines officials is at 11:00."

I tucked my hair behind my ears and rubbed my eyes. Vickie laughed in spite of herself.

"You look like a high school senior who just pulled an all-nighter the day before final exams."

I smiled. "You know how it is when you're meeting with the big guys. I made some major changes last night. Can you take this and type up the revisions? Also, get the graphic and art changes to Andrew and Leslie, and tell them I need the information ready to go no later than 10:15 so we can go over everything before the presentation."

Vickie took the folders from my desk and turned to go.

"You want me to bring in some more coffee?"

I gave her a grateful smile. "Please. Thanks, Vickie."

When she was gone, I rotated my sore neck back and forth and massaged it with my fingers. I hadn't meant to fall asleep at my desk. I usually woke up before the office got buzzing.

Finding me here had shocked Vickie, but it had become routine for me. She didn't know that I had been spending many nights at Turner One, sleeping in my office and dressing in the fully equipped basement bathroom before anyone arrived.

By the time I finished reviewing the Aviator Airlines materials at 3:00 or 4:00 a.m. most days, I saw no sense in driving home only to return a few hours later. So I had begun bringing a change of clothes to the office.

This building was becoming my primary home, and the apartment was my pit stop. Before he left at 9:00 each night, Eduardo, the security guard, would knock on my door and let me know he was locking up.

"You're in charge now, senorita," he'd say and tip his cap.

With Turner One scheduled to present ideas for the Aviator campaign to airline officials today, I had literally been working around the clock to make sure everything was as perfect as could be. There were so many tentacles to this campaign that I had set up an organizational chart in my office to keep everything straight.

Once a design and marketing concept was complete, my staff and I presented each facet to Max Turner for his approval. If he nixed an idea, we made the changes he suggested or went back to the drawing board to come up with something fresher. That happened often enough that we finally began to understand what Max would or wouldn't like before we invested a lot of time in bringing it to life.

"I think we can come up with better copy for the magazine ads," he had said after one group planning session. "They need to be more inclusive of everyone, more family friendly. We want to lure moms and dads and grandparents traveling with their little angels during summer vacation. We want retirees to fly with us to Florida, and business execs to consider us first for their routine commuter flights. Get it?"

Andrew, Leslie, and I wound up devising three targeted ad campaigns, one geared to families, one geared to retirees and vacation travelers, and one tailored to business travelers and first-class flyers.

For the billboard component, Max liked the concept of using pictures of passengers so trusting of the airline that they slept in their airline seats during the flight.

He liked my idea of using a diverse mix of passengers, both ethnic and gender-wise.

"I still think we need a shorter, jazzier catchphrase, though," he had said as he gazed at the mock ads splayed across the table. "We need to hook potential customers quickly and create a slogan that catches on like a wildfire."

The television commercials were a combination of the billboard and print ads, in that they focused on different kinds of fliers, from suited-up professionals and retirees, to college students and young parents.

We planned to use actual passengers in the commercials as they emerged from a flight.

"Since accents are so different across the country, should we shoot a commercial in each region—one for New England, for example, and another for the deep South?" he had asked.

"I don't know about catering to a particular region of the country," I had said slowly, weighing the pros and cons. "It might be humorous and memorable to put people from all over in a single commercial. A man with a Boston accent and a woman with a Louisiana drawl, both applauding the airline's services, could show that we're aiming to meet everyone's needs."

To appease him, I had agreed to create three mini-commercials, one with my idea and the other two with his.

So today was the big day. I was too tired to be nervous, but I knew I had to look my best.

I rode the elevator to the basement and took a long hot shower. I dressed in an olive pantsuit with a silk collared blouse in a lighter, complimentary shade of green.

I had worn this suit late last year when I assisted Myra on revamping the brand of another major American corporation, one Turner One had represented for years. Now here I was, bearing the title that once belonged to Myra, preparing to make my name in the world of advertising. I thought wearing the suit today would give me an added boost of confidence. It was more form-fitting than last year, but I had just about given up on returning to the gym any time soon. I tried to accept the added weight without getting depressed.

Back in my office, I put on matching pumps, pinned a pearl-and-gold butterfly pin to my lapel, and tucked my hair behind my ears to show off my pearl earrings. By the time I applied my makeup and drank my second cup of coffee, I felt ready to take on the world.

There was one other important thing to do. I sat in my chair and pushed it away from the desk. I swiveled away from the door. I bowed my head and closed my eyes, sitting silently for a few minutes before beginning.

Lord, thank you for this day. Thank you for giving me the energy and the creativity to head up this important account. Please be with my team and me today as we meet with the Aviator Airlines staff. Please let them be pleased with this product. In Jesus's name I pray.

I felt better immediately. Still, there was a twinge of guilt for the practice I had developed of calling on God only when I needed something. I rarely took time these days for the morning prayer and meditation I had been determined to incorporate into my routine since the beginning of the year. I knew how empty and stressed-out I felt when I neglected that time. But what was I to do? I had to prove myself with this account.

I told myself once again that I'd do better in lots of areas when this harried process was over. I'd make time to be alone with God, resume my regular exercise schedule, and be available for my friends.

My only reprieve these days had been my blossoming friendship with Micah. He called regularly and met me for quick dinners whenever he could talk me into leaving my desk for an hour in the evenings.

He never lectured me about my schedule or made me feel bad for working through the weekends, even on Sundays. He was there to listen. He offered his opinions sometimes, but in a nonjudgmental way. It was simply the truth, as he saw it through God's lens.

When I had cried on his shoulder about my concerns for Tawana's future and Erika's abusive relationship, I knew that he wouldn't talk about the situations to other people. Instead, he had been blunt with me about my responsibility as a friend.

"God puts people into each other's lives for a purpose. One of the reasons he may have brought you back into Tawana's life at this time is to help her realize that her life isn't over when she becomes a mother. She still has a bright future ahead of her. It will be more challenging to achieve her goals and will probably require that she follow a path with a few more twists and turns, but she can do it. Maybe you're supposed to be her navigator.

"On the other hand, ask yourself what you're learning from this relationship," Micah had suggested. "Maybe Tawana has reappeared in your life to remind you not to take for granted the people in your life and not to ignore situations happening outside of this major account at work.

"And as far as Erika is concerned, I learned in the psychology classes I took in premed and medical school that no amount of pressure from friends or family can force a woman to leave an abusive partner. It's a decision she must make on her own. Most women go back many times before they feel ready to make a clean break. So all you can do is pray for her and offer your unwavering support. Let her know you'll always be there, no matter what."

The advice struck me to my core. Without realizing it, Micah had checked my ego at the door: My friendship with Tawana had nothing to do with me "saving her." God could be using this teenager to reveal his will to *me*. I pondered those revelations for a few days, humbled by how narrow my perspective had been.

Still, even though I felt closer to Micah, I wasn't ready to tell him everything. Would his opinion of me change if he learned that the real reason I pulled away from Tawana, St. Mark's, and everyone else associated with the church was because of my shame over my heritage?

He didn't seem like a shallow person, but then again, I didn't feel like any of my friends were shallow. Yet I didn't want their perceptions of me tainted by my background or want them judging me based on Mama's and Deacon Gates's secret sins.

What would Micah say about the dirty, dark secrets of my past? What would he say about my illegitimacy and my mother's cover-up all these years? I was convinced that even Micah had no pat answers for those deep hurts.

But I do, my child. Come, and I will give you rest.

That voice resonated with me as my phone rang.

I pulled my chair to my desk and pressed the speaker phone.

"It's 10:00," Vickie said, reminding me that very soon, the show would start.

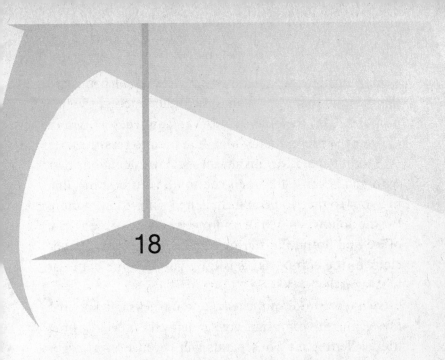

18

I entered the Turner One executive boardroom with Andrew and Leslie flanking me on both sides. We set up our visuals and made sure the overhead projector and videos were ready to go. We tried not to wring our hands while we waited for Max to arrive with Mr. Takahashi, the Aviator Airlines founder and president, and Mr. Connell, the company's vice president.

An hour later, our pitch was finished. We had pulled out all the stops: mock commercials for TV and radio, a signature jingle, and slick magazine and newspaper advertisements.

Mr. Takahashi seemed impressed. He said he was. Apparently, though, he was also a man who knew that the first efforts didn't always equal the best efforts.

"I like what I see. I like this very, very much," Mr. Takahashi told Max. "I'm curious, though, to see what else you can develop. How can we expound on these ideas and make Aviator Airlines a household name?"

Max Turner had done his research. He knew going into the meeting that Mr. Takahashi wouldn't accept the first proposal. I, on the other hand, was stunned.

After the presentation, Max had tried to reassure me.

"I didn't share Mr. Takahashi's style of doing business with you because I wanted you to do your best this first time out so that you could challenge yourself even more for the follow-up," Max told me when he came to my office and found me staring blankly at the grandfather clock in the corner. "This is how you become better at what you do."

Still, I felt sucker-punched. For ten weeks I had poured myself into this campaign, giving up my life, neglecting my friends, letting my houseplants wilt because I was never there to water them and Erika always forgot.

I thought today was the light at the end of the tunnel. Instead, Mr. Takahashi, with Max's permission, was sending me into another chamber of the cave.

During the presentation, I had smiled weakly at Max after Mr. Takahashi had announced his desire to see more material. Max had smiled back and turned to our client.

"Mr. Takahashi, your wish is our command. Serena and her team will give you a dazzling follow-up in, say, three weeks?"

The smile had remained plastered on my face, but I tuned out the rest of the conversation. My thoughts had turned to Imani and how she needed my help even more, now that we were so close to the wedding date. Working on this campaign another three weeks would leave me less time to be there for her before she walked down the aisle.

146

I thought about Tawana, who had asked me last week to serve as her Lamaze coach. Her mother worked nights and didn't seem interested anyway. One of Tawana's supportive teachers had told her that taking the childbirth class might alleviate some of her fears about the changes happening to her body and some of her anxiety over delivering a baby.

Tawana called me at work every so often to be reassured that she was doing the right things to keep herself and the baby healthy. At those times, I thought about calling Mama for advice. She'd know exactly what to tell the girl.

Instead, I would wing it and offer the best advice I could. Give up the sodas. Stay away from the chips and hot dogs as much as possible. Take that multivitamin religiously.

And there was Erika, whom I hadn't talked to in weeks, other than in brief hellos and good-byes as we passed each other on our way in and out of the apartment on the weekends. I could tell she was stressed-out, probably from trying to hide her bruises from her real estate clients.

I also had concerns about her drinking. For the past few weeks, I had been finding empty vodka bottles in the trash. I remembered Micah's advice to hold my tongue, but surely there was more I could be doing to intervene in that situation.

I sighed inwardly. When would the duties associated with this promotion mellow enough to give me time to deal with life?

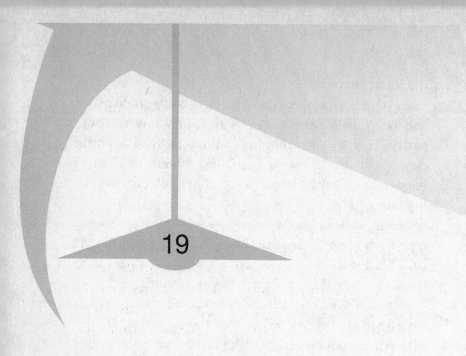

19

I sat at my desk and twiddled my thumbs as I tried to gather my thoughts. I didn't want to think about the work ahead of me right now. I was going to have a brief pity party.

I dialed Erika's number and got her out-of-the-office message. Her cell phone went straight to voice mail, so I figured she was busy. I held the phone and thought for a minute. Whom could I call to wallow in this misery with me?

Micah answered his cell phone on the third ring.

I heard a woman's voice in the background. She was talking and laughing at the same time. This was new.

I knew Micah wouldn't have answered if he had something to hide. My phone number had flashed on his cell phone when it rang.

"Hi, Serena," he said. The depth of his voice still surprised me at times. "How'd the presentation go?"

I rolled my eyes heavenward.

"I'd rather not go into it right now. Thought I'd bore you with the details over dinner tonight."

Micah paused. "Doesn't sound good. But it can't be that bad, right?"

"If you say so . . ."

"Tell you what," he said. "I'm sitting at my place with my mother, trying to decide where to take her for a late lunch. I also want to give her a tour of the infamous Monument Avenue. She wants to see with her own eyes the street that keeps the memory of Confederate heroes alive. In fact, she's trying to convince me to fix her a picnic lunch so we can eat on the median across from the Arthur Ashe statue. Want to ride?"

It dawned on me that I could take the rest of the day off. I had racked up countless hours of overtime and comp time working on this campaign. I deserved a break.

"I can join you in twenty minutes," I said. "But eating at Roseneath and Monument? Ask her if we can stop there just to take pictures in front of the Ashe monument. The dogs taking their afternoon strolls might make it an unpleasant lunch spot, even on a lovely May day like this."

I heard more of the tinkling laughter as Micah relayed my message.

Today my habit of bringing clothes to work for a change after one of my all-nighters would serve me well. I quickly slipped into a pair of jeans and a casual shirt that had been hanging in a small nook of the office.

Instead of driving myself to meet Micah and his mother, we agreed that they would swing by Turner One and pick me up. Micah lived south of the River, in Chesterfield

County, so it made more sense for them to come my way since I was already downtown.

Max and I took the elevator to the first floor together.

"Leaving for the day? Good. Go get your mind off of this morning's presentation. I'm telling you, it was great. This is just how the business works."

I appreciated his encouragement. He knew I was a rookie trying to take my first big disappointment like a pro.

"See you tomorrow, Max. I'll be ready to roll again," I said.

He patted my shoulder as he left for a meeting a few blocks away. I stood just outside the building and enjoyed the warmth of the spring day as I watched for Micah's Jeep.

He swerved into the parking lot a few minutes later. His mother got out and walked over to me with her arms spread wide for a hug.

"How are you, Serena? Micah has mentioned you often. It's nice to finally put such a pretty face with a pretty name."

I tried not to blush as I hugged her. Oklahoma wasn't considered part of the South, but I liked her warm greeting.

I opened the passenger door of the Jeep behind the driver's seat. I slid to the middle seat so I could lean forward and talk comfortably with Mrs. McDaniels as we took off on the brief sightseeing expedition.

"Be sure to put your seat belt on, Serena," Mrs. Mc-Daniels warned. "This boy drives like he wants to eject his mother from the car."

Micah laughed.

"How long are you here?" I asked her as Micah drove toward Monument Avenue. He had told me she was coming for a visit, but I'd been so focused on today's meeting with the airline that I had forgotten she arrived this week.

"I flew in yesterday afternoon, and I'm leaving late tomorrow," she said, turning toward me in her seat. "You know what they say: Fish and houseguests stink after three days."

Micah shook his head.

"That doesn't apply to mothers, you know. You can always change your ticket and stay longer."

She gently patted her son's cheek as he kept his eyes on the road.

"Thank you, dear, but I've got to get back home. Your daddy won't know what to do if he runs out of the meals I cooked and left in the freezer for him. By Friday, he'd be having a cow."

As we laughed, I wondered why Mr. McDaniels hadn't come with his wife. Was he still nursing a grudge about his son's career change?

Mrs. McDaniels seemed to read my mind. She adjusted her glasses on her plump mocha cheeks and turned back toward me.

"Avery hasn't flown a day in his life," she said. "When Micah graduated from college and from grad school, we had to travel to the ceremonies by car. It was the same when my other son got married in Chicago. Now with our baby girl going off to Penn State in the fall, I don't know what we're going to do.

"I decided I couldn't handle a road trip in May and again in August, when we have to help her move. But I wanted to see my big baby, so I got on the plane by myself this time."

She seemed pretty independent for a woman who had decided to put her career as a chemistry professor on hold and raise her children. The way Micah told it, his father had the final say on everything. But Mrs. McDaniels sounded as if she didn't take too much stuff.

When we neared the intersection of Roseneath and Monument, Micah slid into a convenient parking spot and turned off the engine.

"This is the Ashe statue, Mom," he said, pointing to the bronze image of Ashe with a tennis racket raised in one hand and a set of books raised in the other. The sculpture included several children sitting at his feet, gazing up at him with their hands extended.

Mrs. McDaniels seemed oblivious to the cars whizzing by on the busy street as she soaked in the sculpture.

"So this is the source of all the controversy a few years back. The first statue of an African-American to grace this street. It's touching," she said.

We crossed the street and stood on the median just in front of the statue. She snapped some pictures.

I studied her face as she continued to study the statue. Micah resembled her. With her short, layered hair and round features, she was a softer version of him. Based on the family photos I had seen, I thought he looked like his father too.

We left Monument Avenue and headed to Shockoe Bottom, a thriving section of downtown where we quickly were seated at the Tobacco Company restaurant. Mrs.

McDaniels placed her order and turned her attention to me.

"So tell me about yourself, Serena."

The dreaded question. Was I under interrogation? Micah and I were just friends.

Either my face was giving me away or she was really good.

"Don't worry, I'm not sizing you up, dear. I just want to know more about you." She smiled and dug into the mozzarella sticks we had ordered.

I shrugged. "Until my presentation for a major airline this morning, I thought I was a hotshot advertising executive. Now that I've been knocked down a peg or two, I'll revise that to say a hardworking, eager-to-learn advertising executive."

Micah dipped one of the cheese sticks into the marinara sauce. "What happened?" he asked.

I filled them in on my morning, of course leaving out the part about sleeping at the office.

"That sounds like such exciting work," Mrs. McDaniels said. "I don't think you had a setback today; it was a learning experience. You'll look back on this someday and see how much it has helped you grow."

I gave her a grateful smile. Now I knew who had nurtured Micah's wisdom.

She leaned back in the chair and looked at her son. "I didn't give Micah such an easy time when he was trying to make some difficult decisions. But that was because I had already purchased his medical bag to give him when he completed his residency," she said and laughed. Micah must have told her he'd filled me in on his medical school decision. "These days, that expensive bag holds my sewing materials."

Micah looked at her as if she'd lost her mind. "Man," he said, "can I have it and sell it on eBay? I could use the money to help pay off my student loan."

The request didn't faze her. "Sorry, son," she said matter-of-factly. "That bag is serving a purpose." She looked toward me. "Every time I open it to find a scrap of material or a sewing pin, I'm reminded that I don't have the right to chart my own course in life, let alone anyone else's. Micah's dad and I spent more than two hundred dollars on that bag in preparation of handing it over to Dr. McDaniels. We bought it two years early because we were so excited. That was our dream. We were counting down the months. Then God stepped in."

Mrs. McDaniels turned to Micah and looked at him, a tender smile gracing her lips. "The Lord eventually helped me realize that the bag was just a bag. Without the Lord's power with his calling, Micah wouldn't have used it effectively anyway.

"As I sew, I think about the different ways he uses us, and about how what the world may consider the grand prize, God may view in just the opposite way. I decided I want to go God's way."

I nodded in agreement but remained silent. Was my life going God's way?

Mrs. McDaniels changed subjects. "Micah says you're a native of Richmond. Must be nice to have your family nearby."

Micah had never questioned why I hadn't taken him to meet my mother. I'd told him that my father was dead, all the while feeling deceitful. At least when I had uttered those words before, I had believed them to be true.

"This job keeps me so busy that I rarely get to see my relatives," I said as nonchalantly as I could.

Her eyes tried to probe mine. "Yes, I understand," she said. "But there's nothing like having a mother to help you through, to just be there for you. It's so much easier when you're able to see each other without the need to fly or drive for days."

Micah, who sat next to her, gave her a peck on the cheek. "I miss you too, Mom."

She laughed and swatted at his face. "Okay, okay. Enough mushy stuff."

We lingered over our meal, chatting and laughing for more than an hour. We stopped briefly by Maymont Park, and then Micah drove his mother through Carytown.

"How dare you show me these shops and then not let me get out to spend some money!" she said.

Micah rolled his eyes and promised to bring her back the next morning.

By the time they dropped me off at Turner One to pick up my car, the three of us were tired.

"Thanks for helping me get my mind off my disappointing morning," I said to them both as I stepped out of the Jeep.

I reached through the open window and hugged Mrs. McDaniels's neck. I felt like I had made a new friend.

She kissed my cheek.

"Bye, dear," she said. "I enjoyed spending the day with you too. Don't let them wear you down here at work.

There's always more to life than titles and raises and fancy offices. I think you already know that, though."

Micah winked at me and smiled. I waved at him.

"Take care, Mrs. McDaniels," I said. "Have a safe flight home."

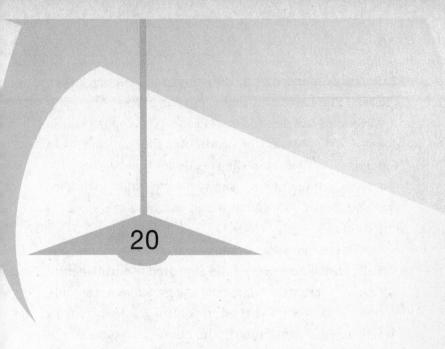

20

I glanced at my watch as I walked toward my car and was surprised to see it was just 4:00. I could still catch Erika at the office and see if she wanted to meet later at Mister P's or maybe somewhere out in Innsbrook.

First, though, I was going home to take a nap. I buckled my seat belt before pulling my cell phone out of my purse and dialing her office number.

Why did her message say she was out for the day? When I'd called her earlier, it was the usual greeting. Erika rarely changed it; only when she knew she would be off work. Had she gotten sick?

I tried her cell phone and still got voice mail. Given her history with Elliott, it was troubling not to be able to reach her.

Erika was lounging on the sofa with the remote control in her hand, watching a talk show, when I came through the door.

Today hadn't been a productive workday for her, either, she said. She had never made it to the office.

At Elliott's insistence, she told me, glancing nervously down the hall toward her bedroom, she had called her supervisor and told him she was under the weather.

"Elliott wanted me to," she said softly, still looking toward her room. "He came by this morning in one of his foul moods."

Then I heard his footsteps.

Erika curled into herself and appeared to shrink before my eyes, a seemingly impossible feat for someone already as tiny as she was. She tried to control her trembling as she heard him come closer. She attempted to mask her fear with a smile.

"Hey, baby," she said weakly when he stood in front of her. "Are you hungry? I can whip up something fast."

Elliott pulled Erika toward him. He squeezed her wrists until she winced.

Doesn't he see me standing here? I thought, appalled at his behavior.

"I just talked to Mavis, and she was *cooing* about you and your offer to help her house hunt. The next time you come by my office, call first," he growled at Erika, obviously so angry that he didn't care if I watched his tirade. "And then, when you arrive, don't come prancing in there like you did Friday, chatting with the secretaries like they're your best buddies. They're secretaries! I'm a lawyer in the firm and trying to make partner. There has to be some protocol!"

Erika kept her head down and nodded.

I stepped to his side, where he could see me as he gripped her. I asked what I knew she had to be thinking.

"Elliott, what are you doing?" I said with as much attitude as I could muster. This was the first time he had roughed her up in my presence. He was really beginning to lose control.

"Let Erika go," I continued. "What in the world is wrong with being nice to another human being, regardless of their job title? Have you forgotten that your mother helped put you through law school on her secretarial salary?"

Elliott's eyes grew wide at my boldness.

"You leave my mother out of this!" he said through clenched teeth. "If she'd never left my father, she wouldn't have had to work so hard. He would have taken care of everything. And I wouldn't have had to settle for my second-choice law school. I would have been at Harvard."

I lost it.

"First of all, you would have had to get *accepted* to Harvard, Elliott. And your mother didn't have to help you pay for the perfectly respectable law school you *did* attend."

He was fuming. His honey complexion was nearly red.

Instead of lashing out at me, he squeezed Erika's wrists tighter, until she yelped in pain.

"Elliott, please don't," Erika begged. "I'm sorry if I upset you. Next time I'll call you before I come by. I won't talk to anyone you don't want me to. It won't happen again."

Elliott clenched his teeth and leaned into her face, nose-to-nose.

"I know it won't, because I'm going to show you the consequences of playing with my future."

The handsome face my friend had fallen in love with was now contorted with anger as he raised his hand to slap her. Erika cowered. Tears streamed down her cheeks. Elliott grew more furious.

Instead of slapping her, he moved his grip to her forearms and squeezed. He knew she could wear a long-sleeved shirt or jacket and no one would be the wiser.

As he punched her in the chest, I began pounding on his back, trying to get him to leave her alone.

"Are you crazy?" I screamed. "Do you think I'm going to let you beat her up in front of me? I'm going to call the police!"

Those words stopped him. He wasn't going to risk his partnership in the law firm by getting a domestic violence arrest on his record. He stepped back, breathing heavily, and stood over Erika's crumpled body.

"If only she would do the right things," he said to me, as if he could explain away his actions. His eyes looked wild. He seemed like another person. "Erika *likes* to anger me."

I ran toward the cordless phone and picked it up, preparing to dial. Erika intervened.

"Serena, please don't," she pleaded from the floor through her tears. "Don't ruin his career. I'm fine. I'm fine, really."

I was crying now too.

"Erika, this has got to stop. Elliott can't do this to you. He's not worth it. You are not an animal he can kick around. This has to stop. And maybe the police are the ones to do it."

Elliott grabbed his coat and walked quickly toward the door, not looking in Erika's direction.

"I can't stay. I've got briefs to review for a big case later in the week. Besides, look what you've made me do," he said, still not looking at Erika as he spoke. "I love you, but I can't have you jeopardizing my career. I've worked hard for this, for me *and* for you."

He left without looking back.

Erika remained on the floor, letting the tears fall. I knelt beside her and wept too.

"Is this what love is about?" she finally asked through her sobs. "Is it supposed to be this ugly and angry and hateful?"

I pulled her to a sitting position and grasped her shoulders. "No, Erika, it's not," I said. "You need to get away from this pompous jerk. God created you to be treated better than this."

But in that moment, I saw in Erika's eyes all the shame, hurt, and fear I'd been feeling about my own circumstances for the last few years. She feared that without Elliott, she wasn't much.

He was a handsome brother with a promising future. And he had picked *her* to spend his time, and his life, with. She couldn't mess this up. He was the only man she had dated and given herself to completely who hadn't used and discarded her.

I bowed my head in defeat when she looked at me and said plaintively, "I love him, Serena. And deep down, I know he loves me."

We hugged, and she continued to cry.

I recalled our days at Commonwealth University and how Elliott had made promises that he would take care of her. She believed him, with his take-charge attitude and his ability to be incredibly sweet to her at times.

Erika hadn't encountered his dark side until our senior year, when he had seen another guy flirting with her at a football game. Elliott hadn't asked any questions. After a hasty trip to his car, he and Erika had returned to the game with her left eye red and watery.

I knew right away what had happened. Erika's wounded-puppy expression said it all. She had tried to downplay the incident, but I wouldn't let her.

"I shouldn't have been talking to that guy," Erika had said.

"Come on, Erika!" I said, trying to control the volume of my voice. "Tell me you don't remember Alvin and how he treated Phylicia freshman year. Like his boxing bag. For six months! All because she thought he was the one for her. You helped her realize what a jerk he was, Erika. Don't tell me you're going to take the same stuff off someone."

Phylicia had been our freshman-year roommate when we had been housed three to a dorm room. For months she had hidden the abuse, but when Erika discovered the bruises one night, Phylicia admitted that Alvin had been hitting her. She swore both of us to secrecy. Somehow she came to her senses and ended the relationship with Alvin. Soon after, she transferred to a college in the Washington, D.C., area.

That day at the game, as I reminded her of Phylicia, Erika had refused to look me in the eyes.

"She was eighteen, Serena," Erika had replied. "Alvin was a cocky football jock. He was just a schoolgirl fling. This is different. Elliott loves me and I love him, and we're going to make a life together. He's a good man."

Elliott had returned to his seat at the game before I could respond to what he had done. He was wearing a wide grin and carrying sodas for himself and his lady. He kissed Erika lightly on the cheek, as if nothing had happened between them half an hour earlier.

"Did something get in your eye, babe?" he said loudly, feigning concern in front of everyone within earshot.

Erika nodded.

"It's nothing," she said a little too brightly. "It'll be fine in a few minutes."

She took the iced drink and snuggled close to Elliott as I angrily watched the rest of the game.

Over the years, I had let Elliott know that I was in on his and Erika's explosive secret. But to keep the peace, Erika had kept as many of the incidents from me as possible. The less I knew, the fewer chances there'd be for me to make the situation worse.

Erika had stuck by her man through college graduation and his decision to enter law school. He had promised when he landed a job at a top firm that she'd become Mrs. Hill. Now he told her he was waiting to make partner.

This afternoon, as we sat there after Elliott had slammed the door on his way out, she, too, had to be remembering that long-ago fall day when the monster had entered their relationship.

She seemed convinced that if she could just be good enough and make Elliott proud of her, the monster would die. Only the sweetest parts of Elliott would remain. Those were the parts she loved and the parts she wanted to spend the rest of her life with.

Erika sighed as she picked herself up from the floor. She wiped her cheeks with the back of her hand.

"At least I didn't lie completely when I told my boss I didn't feel up to working today," she said, trying to make light of the situation.

I want to shake some sense into her, but if Elliott's violent ways don't work, why would mine? I surmised with resignation.

The only thing I know to do is to keep calling on God, the very One she keeps avoiding. I have *to try.*

"Erika, I've had a crummy day too," I said, wiping the remaining streaks of tears from my cheeks. "All my work on this airline account has gotten me is the opportunity to start over and make the campaign 'even better'!"

I gave her a wry smile.

"But some things we can't keep trying in our own power," I said softly. "Erika, God loves you, whether you're willing to acknowledge that or not. He created you, and he loves you no matter what. He sent his Son Jesus to die for us. What makes you think he created you to be hurt like this?

"I know you love Elliott, but the way you're being treated has nothing to do with love. Elliott is obviously full of hurt and anger himself, to have treated you like this all these years. There's nothing you can do to heal him, Erika. You can't love him into being a better boyfriend. Your love can't make his abusiveness disappear."

She turned her back to me and began to weep again. I stood up and walked over to her.

"Erika, you have to love yourself enough to save your-self. If things keep going this way, Elliott is going to kill you. He's not even afraid to hurt you with me here."

She pulled away and sat at the oblong dining-room table, still not speaking. I couldn't stop talking.

"Elliott can't fill that empty place inside you. The only One who can make you fully complete and at peace with yourself is God and his Holy Spirit, Erika. All you have to do is ask him to enter your heart."

She lowered her head onto the table and closed her eyes.

"I need some time alone," she said softly, shutting me out as usual.

I stood there for a moment, gazing at her before I turned and walked toward my room.

To no avail I had pleaded for Erika to call on God, but that didn't mean I couldn't take my own advice. I closed the door to my bedroom and knelt beside my bed. I pressed the palms of my hands together, like I hadn't done since I was an adolescent.

In the semidarkness of the late afternoon, I felt a peace descend on me.

The beautiful thing about talking to God was that I could do it anywhere and anytime. I usually curled up in the up-holstered chair near my bed and raised my eyes heavenward. But today I felt the need to fall on my knees, as I had done when I had learned about Tawana.

I approached him in silence and let the tears flow. Words weren't necessary. God heard the prayers of my heart, for Erika and for myself. He felt our pain—hers over Elliott, mine over the distance I'd created between myself and Mama and my enduring shame at being born of an affair.

Come to me and I will give you rest.

Today, I craved it.

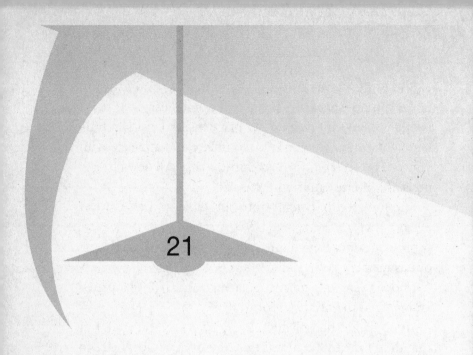

21

When God promised to answer prayer, he never said he would answer it in the ways we'd prefer. When I had asked him to help me find a new church home, I hadn't meant the church I'd left.

I thought about that this morning as I sat in the sanctuary of St. Mark's Baptist Church for the first time in more than five years, watching some of my cousins sing in the young adult choir and seeing all the familiar faces in the pews.

This must be a special Sunday, I thought, because even Brother Isaiah was there. When had he started coming to Sunday worship service? Usually, he just showed up for choir rehearsals during the week and had his own private service during practice: shouting, praying, and all. That generally left his Sunday mornings open for yard work and golf.

Some St. Mark's members seemed startled to see me. I

wondered what Mama had told them about my long absence. Knowing her, not a thing. She would have let them speculate to their heart's content but not have given them a morsel of information they had no legitimate use for.

"Serena's all grown up now and keeping busy with life. She's doing well," would have been her standard response to a "Why don't we see your daughter anymore?" question.

Maybe she would have come closer to the truth with Pastor Taylor, but would she have risked her own reputation and standing in the church? I thought not. As I had learned, even Mama wasn't perfect. She had selfish tendencies just like the rest of us.

Before I could imagine other scenarios for how she had handled my absence, I saw Deacon Gates walk forward with the other church officials to collect offering. Fortunately, he was on the other side of the church. Hopefully he wouldn't notice me as he walked from row to row.

I took the opportunity to look him over from afar. He was tall and still muscular, as if he hadn't long stopped playing college football. The salt-and-pepper of his hair matched his graying mustache. He looked distinguished in a tailored charcoal-gray suit.

He was handsome, I had to admit. Did I resemble him in any way? Had others in church noticed that we favored?

I looked toward the front of the sanctuary and saw Mrs. Gates sitting in her usual spot. She wore a hat of brown and burnt orange that perfectly matched her stylish suit. The girl next to her leaned on her arm as if she were preparing to fall asleep. Kami had to be ten or eleven now.

I had expected to be angry at seeing the Gateses. Instead, I felt sad. By all appearances, they seemed to be the perfect family. How many others sitting in these pews were living with shadows too?

Before my staring could be considered rude, Imani nudged me and pointed out that our cousin was preparing to lead a song for the choir. Zane had a beautiful voice. I had missed hearing him.

Imani smiled broadly as he took the microphone. She had been in Richmond all weekend handling wedding chores and had convinced me to accompany her to St. Mark's this morning. When I had tried to protest, she had outmaneuvered me.

"Look, it's our family church, and I want you there with me. You're my maid of honor. Consider this one of your official duties."

Pastor Taylor was going to ask Imani to stand this morning so he could announce to the congregation that in five weeks she'd be marrying her college sweetheart. Wedding invitations were going in the mail the next day, but the small congregation loved being in the know about what members of the church family were up to.

In the past, I had appreciated how that sense of caring about each other had knit us together. I sometimes wondered now whether that had been the problem for my parents. How had Mama and Deacon Gates gotten so close?

Imani and I talked often in preparation for her wedding, but she had never questioned why I had stopped attending St. Mark's, especially after I returned from grad school. Aunt Jackie and Uncle William must have brought it up, and had probably even asked her if she knew what was going on with me. But it wasn't Imani's style to pry. She'd wait for me to tell her in my own time, if at all.

Or does Imani already know my reasons? I wondered as the pianist played the opening chords of "We Fall Down" by Donnie McClurkin. *Somebody* knew Mama's and Deacon Gates's nearly thirty-year-old secret.

I had decided this morning to put aside my own issues and honor Imani's request, primarily because I still hadn't learned how to tell the girl no. And she knew it.

I returned my attention to the service as Zane closed his eyes and started singing.

"We fall down, but we get up. We fall down, but we get up. We fall down, but we get up. For a saint is just a sinner who fell down . . ."

By the time Pastor Taylor stood in the pulpit to deliver his sermon, I felt the Holy Spirit's presence in the church. It felt so good to be home, in the house of the Lord. It felt wonderful to receive the Word of God again and feel as though through the preacher's message, God was speaking directly to me.

The sermon that morning was from 2 Kings, about a woman whose son was deathly ill. When Elisha, a prophet of God, sent his servant to ask her if everything was all right, the woman proclaimed, "It is well"—even though her only son had died suddenly just hours earlier.

"It was as if she knew by being asked the question 'Is your child all right?' that it meant her child would be healed," Pastor Taylor said. His fervor seemed to shake the rafters of the sanctuary. "She was speaking her desires, her prayers into existence. She had the faith, and she put it into action. Sure enough, when that woman returned home, the prophet came with her and through the power of the Lord, breathed life back into her son.

"How many of us trust God enough to try him like that?" Pastor Taylor questioned, to loud responses from the congregation. "How many of us can lay down our reasoning and just go with God's flow? No matter what we're facing, if we'll just give it to God, we, too, can say with confidence that 'It is well!' We, too, can lay down our burdens and not worry about having to micromanage situations until we can come up with a solution!

"God is the solution to all that ails us. He provides mercy, he provides grace, he provides forgiveness. All we have to do is claim it and declare that it is well!"

Tears trickled down my face as I listened. "Yes, Lord," I prayed. "I know it can be well if I'll just release this anger and shame. But how do I do that?"

Imani offered me a tissue. I took it and tried to repair some of the damage to my face.

My heart was full. God had never left me; I had simply held him at bay. I knew he would help me sort everything out, if I'd just let him.

After Pastor Taylor wrapped up the sermon, he asked Timony, a woman I had grown up with in the choir, to sing the hymn "It Is Well."

Thanksgiving began to overflow in the place. One by one, people began coming forward to share testimonies of how God had blessed them. This wasn't a usual part of St. Mark's service as I remembered it, but Pastor Taylor never quashed the flow of the Holy Spirit. Whenever people wanted to praise God or give him thanks, Pastor Taylor joined them.

Sister Jones started off the praise reports. She had recovered from a brain aneurysm and was now helping other afflicted adults who were undergoing therapy to regain some of their physical abilities.

After years of trying to bear children, Pam and Mark Cyphus had adopted two-year-old twin boys three months ago. They had found out last week that Pam was pregnant.

The Carters thanked God for saving them from the brink of divorce.

"We didn't think we'd make it, but God is so good," Mr. Carter said. "He put a new love in our hearts for each other. He transformed our habit of taking each other for granted into a beautiful love song, where after fifteen years of marriage, we're more in love than ever before. We are living proof that God can do anything!"

I praised God along with the members who shared their experiences.

And then came Mama.

The church fell silent as she walked forward to take the microphone.

"Some of you have asked about my weight loss and my frequent absences from service, but as many of you know, I'm a private person," she began as I watched, unable to shift my gaze from her face.

Had she seen me here in the audience today? Was she about to embarrass me—us—by confessing her sins with Deacon Gates?

My fears were unwarranted. But what she said stunned me.

"That privacy has allowed me to undergo chemotherapy

and radiation with dignity for months." She gave a half smile. "Some of you thought I'd suddenly become fascinated with hats, but Pastor Taylor and my sister-in-law, Jackie, knew I started wearing them to hide my bald spots.

"Now it's time to put pride aside. The heavenly Father said the prayers of the righteous availeth much, and as I battle for my life, I need your prayers.

"I was diagnosed with colon cancer six months ago. The initial two months of chemo and radiation removed all traces of the disease. But tests last month showed a new spot has developed.

"Just as this disease is aggressively attacking me, I'm aggressively claiming my healing. And I'm openly asking for your prayers for my healing."

Mama's voice faltered at the end, and she lowered her head. Pastor Taylor took the microphone from her and hugged her.

Imani turned to me, wide-eyed, and squeezed my hand.

"Why didn't you tell me, CeCe? You've been helping me plan a wedding and Aunt Vi has been this sick?"

My tears kept me from responding. She searched through her purse for another tissue.

Guilt and anguish flooded through me.

Mama has been staring down death, and my pride and anger have kept me from being there for her. How could I have let this happen?

Still holding on to Mama, Pastor Taylor turned to the congregation.

"You heard Sister Jasper. She needs our prayers. She is

right: The prayers of the righteous availeth much. Where at least two believers come into agreement over a matter before God, he hears and answers our petitions. Let us come in support of this sister. We're going to pray her through this affliction, starting right now."

Members of the congregation rose to go forward and surround Mama as Pastor Taylor prepared to pray.

I was too afraid to speak, fearful that the tears would start afresh. I simply squirmed through the crowd until I reached Mama.

I touched her elbow, and she looked up. Her startled reaction told me she hadn't seen me earlier. She pulled away from Pastor Taylor and leaned toward me for a hug. Both of our tears started afresh.

"I'm sorry, Mama," I sobbed in her ear. "I'm here now. You aren't in this alone."

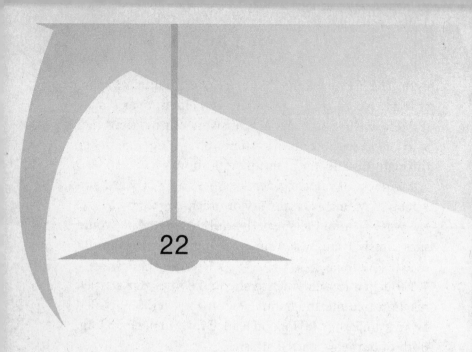

22

As I sat across from Mama at dinner that afternoon, I realized how thin she had gotten.

I couldn't stop the waterfall of tears. Imani, who sat next to me at the table, kept passing me tissues between bites of her mother's roast and mashed potatoes.

Mama didn't say much. She just kept smiling at me and shaking her head. "Is that really you across the table from me?"

Aunt Jackie had insisted that we come over, but right now, I really wanted to be alone with Mama so I could fall at her feet and beg her to forgive me. How could she still love me when I had treated her so harshly?

I knew we'd have time later that night to discuss those things. I tried again to compose myself.

"Get used to seeing me," I said softly and smiled at her.

Mama leaned forward and squeezed my hand. Her fingers were so cold.

"It will be my pleasure, baby," she said and looked into my eyes.

Imani had helped speed things along at dinner and urged us to leave right after dessert.

"Mom, you know they have a lot to talk about, so let's let them go. And you and I can do some final wedding planning," she told my aunt.

The mention of the wedding saved the day. Aunt Jackie was consumed by the tiniest details. She hugged Mama tightly and me too.

"It was good to see you in church today, Serena. Come back home soon, you hear?"

I smiled but didn't answer.

"Oh, Jackie, home is wherever her heart is," Mama answered on my behalf and smiled.

Imani hugged me and whispered in my ear, "Don't let Mom bother you. You do what God's telling you to do, CeCe. And just take care of your mother. That's what is important now. The wedding stuff is up to speed. I'll be fine."

Fresh tears formed as I hugged her back.

"Just pray, Mani, just pray."

She held me away from her and looked into my eyes.

"I've been doing that for years, CeCe. God answered a prayer today."

I followed Mama, who was already walking to her car. When we reached her house, I pulled into the driveway behind her.

She stood waiting for me in the doorway as I locked

my Audi and mentally kicked myself for being so proud when I bought it on my third anniversary at Turner One. Suddenly, the car and other material things didn't matter much.

I surveyed my childhood home as I walked toward Mama. It looked the same, but the paint was peeling in some places, and the porch had a rickety step. I made a mental note to get that repaired as soon as possible so Mama wouldn't suffer an accidental fall.

When I reached her, she stepped aside and motioned for me to come in. As soon as she closed the door, she let the tears fall that she had held at bay at Aunt Jackie's.

"Welcome home, Serena. I missed you."

We fell into each other's arms and cried. She was so thin. I could feel the bones on her back. It made me weep harder.

I was losing my mama.

When we finally composed ourselves, we sat across from each other on the familiar beige sofa and love seat in the living room. She spoke first.

"As I walked forward during the service this morning, I was asking God why he wanted me to publicly share an illness I had already battled on my own for six months. Part of the answer was what I said before the congregation: I do need their prayers. But now I know, it was also to bring you back into my life.

"When you touched my elbow and I turned and saw you, I thought I was going to pass out. It was confirmation from God that he's going to answer my prayers. I've been praying for you to return to my arms for a long, long time, Serena."

"Mama," I said, my voice trembling, "I don't know what to say."

I didn't want to dampen this moment by bringing up my hurt and shame over her affair with Deacon Gates and the lie I had lived most of my life regarding my father. That wound was still raw, but right now Mama needed me to be there for her, regardless of what had gone on between us before.

That past mattered, but then again, it didn't. I understood today that no matter what, she was still my mama. I loved her, sin and all.

Just as I love you.

Yes, Lord, just as you do, I said silently.

"I'm home, Mama," I said. "I'm here. We're going to get through this together."

I couldn't apologize yet for my absence, even though I felt guilty that she was sick and I hadn't known. I asked God to give me the strength to do the right thing.

My grace is sufficient for you . . .

"I'd like to move back in and help you through this," I said softly.

The emotions that crossed her face filled me with more tears. There was surprise, uncertainty, gratitude, and love. Her expression seemed to ask, "You still love me after all, don't you?"

"Are you sure?" she asked tentatively. "Don't bite off more than you can chew, Serena. During my last round of chemo and radiation, a home health nurse came by three times a week to make sure I was doing okay."

I shook my head.

"You won't need one this time. I'll be here to take care of you and the house."

She smiled as fresh tears coursed down her cheeks. She sat on the sofa across from me, but I could tell she wanted to touch me.

I stood up and leaned across her small coffee table to hug her.

"Call me Nurse Serena," I said, trying to lighten the mood. But she remained serious.

"Thank you, baby. Thank you."

"Thank you for letting me do it, Mama."

23

By the time I made it to the apartment that evening after 8:00, I was drained. But I had so much to do that I couldn't settle down.

There was work to think about, but more immediately, I had to talk to Erika about our joint lease. I'd continue to pay my part of the rent as long as Turner One didn't fire me, I decided.

I hoped I wasn't about to cause Erika too much anxiety.

I found her in the living room sitting on the floor. The riffs of Jill Scott boomed from the CD player as she flipped through bridal magazines.

She looked up and smiled.

"Go to church for the first time in years and can't get out of there, huh?"

She turned off the music when she saw my expression.

"Everything okay?"

My eyes were red-rimmed, but I had no more tears left.

Or so I thought. As I began to talk, I felt them coming. I sat on the sofa and looked down, speaking softly.

"I found out at church this morning that Mama has cancer. Colon cancer. It's aggressive, and she's about to undergo a second round of chemotherapy and radiation."

I looked up as Erika gasped. She came over and hugged me. "Serena, I'm so sorry. What are you going to do?"

"That's what I need to talk to you about," I told her. "I need to be there for Mama, at least this time. She went through the first round of treatments on her own. I need to see her through this, Erika. That means I need to move in with her."

Erika nodded. "Go to your mother. I'll figure things out here."

She was being kindhearted. We both knew that because I earned more, I paid a larger portion of the rent in return for her cooking most of the meals and paying a majority of the utility bills. There was no way she could swing the rent on her own. And I doubted that she'd want to bring in a new roommate.

"What I'm proposing to do is to continue paying my part of the rent as long as I can," I said. "I don't want to leave you hanging, and technically, this will still be my home. I'm just moving back to the city for a while to help Mama. As long as Turner One gives me paid leave, we should be fine for the duration of her treatment."

Erika protested. "Serena, you can't pay rent here and live somewhere else. That's crazy. And you may need the money to help your mother. Why don't I check into getting out of the lease on the basis of your mother's medical emergency or try to find a temporary roommate?"

I didn't like the idea of someone else invading my space, even temporarily. And what if I wanted to come back in three months, when Mama was well again? I was already claiming her return to good health. Mama was strong. God would deliver her.

"Let's try it my way for a while and see what happens, okay?"

Erika eventually relented. "Whatever you need me to do, consider it done. Don't hesitate to ask. I'll help cook and clean for Ms. Jasper. I'll run errands for you or whatever you need. I love your mother too."

We hugged each other tightly.

I sat back and looked into her eyes.

"If you've ever considered talking to God, now's the time to do it," I told her solemnly. "Because if you believe in God, you believe in his power to heal. And if you believe in that power, you can pray for him to extend a miracle to Mama."

Erika cast her eyes downward and didn't answer. I knew that meant she wasn't ready to go the spiritual route.

I stood up and changed the subject. "I'm going to pack some things that I'll need, but I'll be coming back and forth a lot. Mama starts a new round of chemo on Tuesday, and I want to be somewhat settled at the house before then."

Erika looked up at me. "I don't know what kept you two apart for so long, but I'm glad to see you've found your way back to each other. What you two had was special."

I nodded and began walking toward my room. The bridal magazines on the floor caught my eye again, and I turned to her.

"What gives?"

She smiled sheepishly and walked over to me, her left hand extended.

There sat a diamond, almost as large as Erika's entire palm, on her fourth finger.

"Oh my goodness," I said slowly, enunciating each word. I reached for her hand. "How big is this Rock of Gibraltar?"

"Two carats!" Erika exulted. "Elliott asked me to marry him this morning over brunch at the Jefferson. He'll be named a partner in the firm by the end of the year."

"Oh my goodness." I couldn't utter anything else. The ring was beautiful, but in my heart, I knew it didn't accurately reflect their relationship.

I hugged her tightly and remembered Micah's advice to just be there for my friend. I couldn't make decisions for her, but I could love her in spite of her choices.

After I hugged her we sat on the floor and rifled through the magazines.

"So how soon after the proposal did you raid the store?" I joked.

As she sat back Indian style, I noticed a purplish bruise on her cheek, mostly hidden with foundation.

I tried to keep my tone lighthearted. "What happened to your cheek? Bought the wrong shade of blush?"

Erika laughed nervously and looked away. "Girl, you know how clumsy I am. I've got to be careful not to walk into any doors before my wedding day."

"Or any fists," I said softly.

Erika frowned. "Serena, don't start. I know Elliott isn't your favorite person, but can't you just be happy for me?

I'm a big girl. I know what I'm doing and whom I love. I know that Elliott loves me."

Her defiance deflated my attitude. Too much had gone on today for me to be so contrary. I just didn't have it in me.

Maybe Erika was right. She knew exactly what she was getting into. She was making the wrong choice, as far as I was concerned, but I had no right to treat her like a child and tell her how to live.

And I knew Micah was right. I needed to be there for my friend whenever she decided to leave Elliott. If she ever did. All I could do was continue to pray that she would be strong enough to walk away.

Even as I agreed to serve as Erika's maid of honor, I silently asked God to do what he thought best to move Erika out of danger and into a closer walk with him.

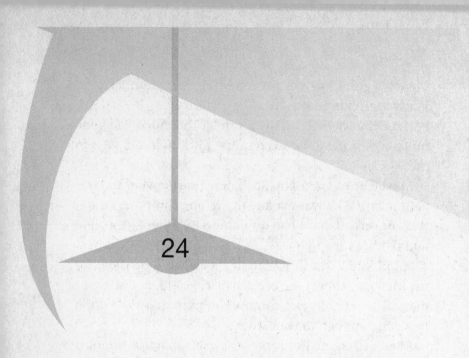

24

It was the hardest decision I'd ever had to make, yet it was almost easy. I was at peace with my choice.

In the middle of the biggest account of my career, when I'd been given three weeks to prove my mettle, to show the advertising world that I was among the industry's best and brightest, I was on my way out the door.

Trust in me with all your heart, and lean not on your own understanding. In all your ways acknowledge me, and I will direct your paths.

I no longer considered that inner voice a nagging reminder of what I should be doing. I finally accepted it for what it was all along—God's Holy Spirit nudging me in the right direction.

So this morning I sat in Max Turner's office, resolved that no matter what happened, God was going to get me through this and work the entire situation out for my good. I didn't waste time with small talk.

"Thanks for meeting with me this morning, Max. I've made a difficult decision in the past twelve hours that I hope you'll understand."

He looked at me expectantly.

"My mother has colon cancer, and she needs my help. I know we're wrapping up the final changes to the Aviator Airlines campaign, with ten days to go before we meet with Mr. Takahashi again. But I've got to be there for my mother. I need to take an extended leave of absence."

Max rose from his chair and walked around to the front of his desk.

"Serena, I'm so sorry. How's your mom doing? What's the prognosis?"

"We're not certain, at this point. She underwent chemo and radiation a few months ago, and hoped that had killed all the cancerous cells. But a couple of weeks ago, she learned that the cancer has returned. She's fighting for her life, and I need to be there."

Max nodded. "No question about it."

But then he fell silent. I could tell he was torn between giving me his blessing to go and asking me to continue working on the account. "Well, you've done enough re-working of the Aviator account that Andrew and Leslie should be able to make revisions in time for our meeting with Mr. Takahashi," he said thoughtfully. "I'm just concerned that your final touch will be missing. You've worked so hard on this; I want you to see this through all the way if you can.

"Is there any way you can come in on the days that your mom is not undergoing treatment? The company will pay for a nurse to sit with her during that time."

His offer touched me and at the same time appalled me. *No nurse could take my place,* I thought indignantly. But I also considered all the work I had put into the campaign.

Hadn't I entered this office at peace with my decision to leave it all behind? Why isn't this going as I had planned?

I sighed and shook my head, indicating that I didn't have an immediate answer for him.

"Thanks for your offer to help, Max. But I just don't know yet. I need to talk to my mother and see what she prefers. And I probably should talk to her doctors too, to see just how much help she'll need during the treatment. If I need to be there for her constantly, I guess I'll have to be. But I hope you know that I also value my job and this company. You've been wonderful to me, and I don't want to leave you hanging. Can I have a couple of days to sort everything out?"

Max glanced at the calendar before responding. I knew he was calculating how much time that would leave us to finish the changes on the Aviator Airlines campaign.

He was a good man, but he also had a company to run.

"Can we touch base on Thursday?" he asked.

"Certainly," I answered, trying to keep frustration from seeping into my tone.

I had expected to obtain a leave of absence without any drama. But to be fair, Max had told me from the beginning how important this Aviator Airlines campaign was to the company. He hadn't been joking.

This one, I would really have to pray on.

Trust in the Lord . . .

I rose and shook Max's hand.

186

"Thank you, Max, for everything. I'll leave my mother's phone number with your secretary so you can reach me if you need to before Thursday. And I'll spend today bringing Andrew and Leslie up to speed on the changes to the campaign so they'll be prepared to proceed, based on what you and I decide later in the week."

Max squeezed my hand.

"I'm sorry to be so callous about this, Serena. I wish I could send you on your way with no worries. But you know what the Aviator Airlines account could mean for Turner One. We'll get through this together. Your mother is in my prayers. My family and I will be lifting her up."

With that, he walked me to the door and asked his secretary, Marla, to get my mother's number.

Because Mama wouldn't start chemo until tomorrow, I planned to get as much work done as I could today. I pulled together all of my notes on the Aviator campaign and asked Andrew and Leslie to clear their schedules for a long lunch meeting.

Mama called just as I wrapped up the two-hour session with Andrew and Leslie. I had left them fully informed on the areas of the campaign presentation I had been handling.

I hadn't told Mama about my plans to take a leave of absence or about the major project I'd been working on for months, but she seemed to know that something important was going on at work. Maybe she could still read me better than I could understand myself.

It felt good to have her calling again just to talk. The conversation was a little awkward, but I knew we'd grow comfortable with each other soon. We both wanted that.

"Serena, I know you're really busy—you always used to be when it came to your work," she said.

I realized that she'd never been part of my full-fledged career, only my internships and advertising studies. *If only she knew just how harried the pace can get,* I thought.

"I was calling to see what time you planned to come over tonight. If you're coming in time for dinner, I'll try to have something ready."

I couldn't believe her.

"Now, Mama, at some point the Southern hospitality has to be put to rest. I mean, after all, I'm your daughter. There's no need to entertain me. I'll be over around 7:00 with dinner in hand, already prepared—by a local restaurant," I said and laughed. "And a friend is coming with me. I hope that's okay."

Mama laughed too. I heard a lightness in her voice that had been missing for a long time.

"Are you coming back to rule my roost, Miss Thang?" she said. "And who's this friend? Someone other than Erika?"

"You'll see, Mama," I said and rolled my eyes. She was going to faint when she met Micah.

She laughed again and then turned serious.

"I also wanted to give you a call, Serena, because I know you're probably thinking about taking time off work to care for me. I wanted to ask you not to put your work on hold for me. Just your presence here in the evenings will be helpful. I can still get a nurse to sit with me a couple of afternoons each week if I need one. My insurance will cover that. Otherwise, I'll be fine. Just having you back in my life is medicine enough."

The lump in my throat kept me from responding for a few minutes. My grip on the telephone receiver tightened as I attempted to compose myself.

"But I've been gone so long, Mama. I really want to be there for you," I said in a near whisper, my voice trembling. "Work can wait. We have a lot of catching up to do."

Her voice was softer too. "We do, baby. But I've been talking to Imani and your Gram about you all these months. I know you're working on a major account for your company, one that could take you to places you've dreamed about ever since you wanted to enter this profession. I'm not going anywhere. You do what you have to at work, and we'll manage everything else the best we can. I mean that."

Mama hadn't changed. She would probably always put my needs before her own, even after I had treated her so badly.

"I'll do whatever I need to do to be there for you, Mama. But thanks for your support."

I got up and locked the door to my office when we ended the call. I knelt at my chair and bowed my head.

Lord, here I am, standing in need of your love, mercy, grace, and guidance. I don't know how I've made it this long without you, but I've been humbled enough in the past twenty-four hours to know that I was foolish to try.

I need you more than ever now to direct my paths. Lord, please hear my cry and send an answer. Help me choose the right thing to do. I messed things up so badly between Mama and me that I don't want to squander any of our precious time by being here when I should be there, or being there so much that I'll be overbearing.

You tell me what to do, Lord. You work out all the details, and I promise to follow through.

I rose and sat at my desk with my eyes closed for a few minutes more. It felt so good to take it all to God.

Even though I'd pushed him away, he was still there, waiting to scoop me up again. I shook my head in wonder.

"Nobody but God," I said aloud.

My final answer about what to do hadn't come yet, but I knew that for today, I had more than enough other loose ends to tie up.

One of my chores was the difficult phone call I'd have to make to Tawana. I had promised a few months ago to serve as her Lamaze coach and had done a fairly good job of keeping that commitment. I'd missed the fourth class, which had left her angry and feeling abandoned. But it couldn't be helped. Max had requested more changes to an idea I had for the campaign, and I had to pull an all-nighter to get the information to him at 9:00 the next morning.

"You're no different than my baby's daddy!" Tawana had spat at me through her tears when I called her about an hour before the Lamaze class and told her I wasn't going to be able to make it. "I can't rely on you or anyone else. All of y'all are the same."

I had listened and let her fume. She had a right to be angry. Even I, the one person she looked up to, couldn't be there when she felt she needed me the most. But I knew that Max needed my work too. I had to honor his request.

Remembering that incident as I dialed Tawana's home number, I knew this call wouldn't be any easier.

As soon as I told her that I had asked my cousin, Tia, also a member of St. Mark's, to serve as her Lamaze coach, she began sighing heavily. Tia had worked with the youths for as long as I had, and Tawana knew her fairly well. Still, Tawana wasn't happy with the last-minute switch.

"I hope you know that I wouldn't leave you so close to delivery like this if my mother weren't so sick, T," I said. "I need to be available to her at all times. And I don't want you to go into labor and have me not show because my mother is ill and needs me. I'll still go to class with you and Tia, but just in case I can't make it to the birth, you won't have to worry about being alone."

She tried to be polite.

"I guess I understand. I don't know why I thought someone as important as you could be there for me anyway. You moved on a long time ago, when you went to Boston. I should have gotten the message."

I wanted to protest, but how else could she have viewed my abrupt absence from her life and from the church I had encouraged her to consider a safe haven, a second home?

"Tawana, I'm sorry if I hurt you when our friendship fizzled before. I was dealing with some personal issues that led me to stay away from church. Now that I look back, I can see that I didn't handle things in the best way. I thought running away was the answer, but it wasn't. I'm sorry if in my running, I abandoned you. But that's not what I'm trying to do now. I promise that as soon as Mama is well, I'll be coming by to help out with the baby."

I knew that she'd blow off my promises until I proved them. I didn't blame her.

My next call was to Micah to fill him in on what had happened since I'd talked to him on Saturday. He confirmed our plans to meet me that night at my mother's house so he could pray with us and join us for dinner.

"You know you're doing the right thing, right?" he asked when I explained that I was leaning toward taking a leave of absence. "Even though this is the campaign of your career, this is also a crucial point in your relationship with Christ.

"The choices you make right now, the issues and people you prioritize right now, are reflective of where your heart is," he said.

I looked at him but didn't respond. I knew he was right. Why was I even struggling over this?

"Maybe you need to take a break from work and focus on your mother," Micah said. "If somehow you can wrap up this campaign and still do that, cool. If not, God has something else in mind."

I nodded even though he couldn't see me.

Micah still didn't know about all the hurt I'd felt at Mama these past few years or the questions that I still wanted answered. But he was right.

Now was the time and season to resolve all of this. It took something as terrible as Mama getting cancer for me to appreciate the need to come to some resolution, but at least Mama was freely welcoming me back into her home and her heart.

With all the time we'd been apart, we had a lot of catching up and forgiving to do. That wouldn't be possible with twelve-hour workdays devoted to Aviator Airlines.

I felt, for the first time in a long time, that my mama was worth the sacrifice. The answer to my dilemma was becoming crystal clear.

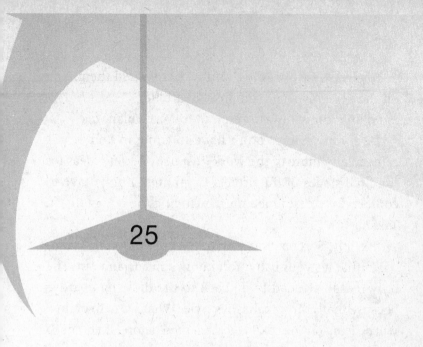

25

The answers weren't as clear for Max. He finally admitted that he wanted me to lead the team in completing the Aviator Airlines project.

"You can work from home as much as you like and come in only when we hold decision-making meetings about the final direction of the campaign," he said. "That means you'll still direct and oversee the project, but others on staff will do the hands-on work. And when Mr. Takahashi comes in again, you can do the presentation for him. That way, you're still on the payroll, and you'll have more time after the campaign for your leave of absence. What do you think, Serena?"

Max had called me Wednesday morning as I sat perusing the newspaper at Mama's house. The chemo treatment the day before had left her with nausea and diarrhea, and she hadn't gotten much sleep during the night.

Finally, she was resting fitfully. I answered the phone on the first ring so it wouldn't disturb her.

I didn't know how to respond to Max's plan.

"Are you saying I don't have to come in and physically do any more of the work, just okay or veto ideas for the final stages of the project by phone? I only have to come in for certain meetings, including the one with Mr. Takahashi?"

"Exactly, Serena. You've worked enough on this campaign that it's your baby. You know it inside and out. The only reason we had to go back to the drawing board is because that's Mr. Takahashi's style. What we deliver now will be icing on the cake you presented before. If you need to see the changes in progress, a courier can drop off copies every day, once a week, or whenever you prefer, as you work around your mother's schedule."

Thank you, Lord. The decision had been made for me.

"Max, I can't thank you enough for going to all of this trouble," I said. "When my mother is better, my full attention is Turner One's again. And in the meantime, I'm still going to do my best to make the Aviator Airlines campaign sing. This contract is ours, I already know it."

By the time I got off the phone with Max, Mama had shuffled into the kitchen and was making a pot of coffee.

"Sit down and let me do that for you," I scolded.

"Are you going to baby me the whole time you're here?" she asked, as if annoyed.

I hesitated before being truthful. "As much as I can, yeah."

She pretended to glare at me and then laughed.

"Good! I like it black." She sat at the table and picked up the newspaper.

I laughed too and got to work.

"Was that your boss on the phone?" she asked as she perused the front page.

"Yes, that was him." I turned to her, eager to share the plan that had been worked out.

"Those folks must really love you," she said when I explained how I'd keep working to complete the project by the end of next week.

I shook my head in wonder.

"I don't know, but I love Max Turner," I said. "He's always been a great boss. Today, my respect for him soared to a new level."

Mama decided to switch gears.

"Speaking of love, what's going on with you and the young man who graced us with his presence last night? Where did you find *him*? Imani hasn't said a word!"

Mama had given Micah a light hug when he walked through the door last night carrying two bouquets of flowers—one for me and for her.

She had winked at me as she hurried off to find vases for the daylilies. I knew that meant she thought he was cute.

Over the greens, cornbread, and tender chicken and rice I had ordered from Ma-Musu's, a local Liberian restaurant, both of them had bragged about their chess skills and challenged each other to a game.

"Better yet, young man, how 'bout a simple round of checkers?" Mama had offered. "You better start there so I won't whip you on our first meeting!"

Mama didn't eat much of the mildly spicy food, but the conversation and laughter seemed to fill her.

I had sat at the table and chuckled with them, taking it all in. It was good to see Mama focused on something other than her condition. I was touched that she and Micah were so at ease with each other.

And he had been "gracious enough," he said, to let her win all three rounds of checkers.

"Is Imani your 'Serena spy'?" I asked this morning. "She hasn't said anything because she hasn't met Micah yet. I'll have to tell you the long version of how we met soon, but the important part is that he's a thoughtful person with a kind spirit who just happens to be gorgeous."

"Well, are you two an item?" Mama prompted.

I laughed. "I guess you could say we're dating, but right now it's nothing exclusive. He's someone I can talk to about anything and get the kind of wisdom and spiritual guidance I need versus having someone say what he thinks I want to hear. It's wonderful."

Mama's eyes got misty.

"That's the first time I've heard you talk about a man in quite that way. I can tell he's someone special. You keep bringing him around, 'cause he sho' ain't hard to look at!"

I had to laugh. The cancer was sapping her strength, but Mama's spirit hadn't changed a bit.

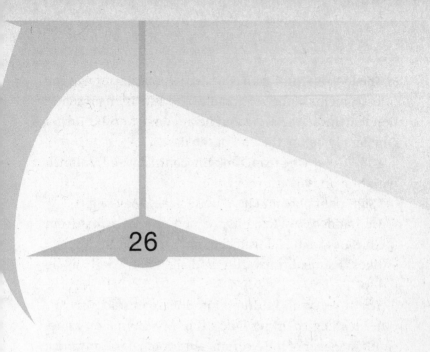

26

The next eight days flew by.

On June sixth, I sauntered into the large board-room at Turner One and wowed Mr. Takahashi with my revamped presentation. He smiled when I unveiled the airline's new brand: "Aviator Airlines—You're Flying with Family."

The tagline in the radio and television ads would be, "You don't need to earn your wings, we're flying for you."

He sat up straighter in his chair as I described the website changes, including an interactive map that would allow prospective passengers to click on a destination city where Aviator Airlines flew and get detailed flight information, as well as be linked to other supporting businesses such as rental car agencies and hotels. Throughout the pages, visitors to the site would be urged, "Choose Aviator and you won't go wrong. That's because you're flying with family."

The look on Mr. Takahashi's face as I went through the final segments of the print, radio, and television presentation convinced me he would be a member of the Turner One family before the end of the day.

Our Turner One team took the contract to a late lunch with him and his attorneys.

"Sign right here and it's a done deal," Max said.

He handed Mr. Takahashi a pen as I sat across from the businessman and watched him make the appropriate strokes. I smiled outwardly and sighed inwardly as he did so.

The three-year, multimillion dollar contract was another feather in Turner One's cap. My reputation as account manager of the effort meant I could name my price at Turner One and, for that matter, at just about any ad agency I desired.

A story in this month's issue of *Advertising USA* about my talent and about the creative endeavors I undertook to land the Aviator account had only raised my profile in the industry. But for now, I was content. Max had been wonderful about giving me flexibility so I could work around Mama's needs. I was truly grateful for that.

I had told Micah to be on standby, ready to attend Turner One's celebration reception with me tomorrow if I landed the account. On my way home from the deal-making lunch with Aviator Airlines officials, I called and told him to pull his tux out of his closet. We'd be going to the Shockoe Bottom Arts Center.

I spent the rest of the evening watching cowboy show reruns with Mama. She loved them; they put me to sleep.

Before I knew it, "tomorrow" had arrived. All morning

I was busy getting my hair washed and styled and getting an overdue manicure and pedicure. Because of too many missed trips to the gym, I was forced to push several semi-formal dresses to the back of the closet and go shopping.

Now that this campaign was over, I promised myself, I was going to get myself back into shape. I had been foolish anyway to let work so consume me that I began to let myself go. Looking back, I realized no job was worth my health and sense of well-being. What would the job do for me if I became ill and couldn't meet deadlines or stay creative?

You cannot serve two masters . . .

I understood now what God had been saying.

When we arrived at the reception later that night, Micah teased me about being the star of the evening, especially after our entrance was greeted with applause.

My co-workers approached me, one by one, throughout the night to congratulate me.

"So what did you do to land this account anyway?" Clark Bridges asked, swilling champagne around his glass before sipping loudly. "What made Max choose you?"

Because I was used to the competitiveness of this business, I wasn't taken aback. I smiled.

"Commitment and hard work are sometimes rewarded with a challenging project," I said, almost pointedly.

By the end of the evening, I was exhausted.

I had tossed and turned at bedtime all week, fretting about how Mr. Takahashi would receive the revised campaign. As usual, I had arrived at the office at 6:30 a.m. yesterday and tried to memorize as much of the campaign spiel as I could before the big meeting.

Then we had the meeting and lunch afterward. And today had been consumed by my efforts to get ready for tonight. I was so tired I felt like I was sleepwalking.

Micah comfortably chatted with the advertising execs from Turner One and with their respective dates. He wasn't eager to leave or wanting to stay longer. He clearly made the night about me; I was making all the decisions.

When I was nearly ready to crawl into a corner and take a nap, I nodded, and he grabbed my hand and led me toward the door. Max stopped us in the art center's foyer.

"Serena, your paid leave of absence can begin tomorrow, okay? And when you return, we'll firm up details about making you account manager of the Aviator Airlines campaign for the next three years. Thanks for all of your hard word, kid. Have a good evening!"

He patted me on the back and walked away before I could respond. Micah and I stared at each other.

"Sounds like a permanent promotion to me," he said and grinned.

I smiled weakly as my stomach began to tremble.

Is this what I really wanted? The party had been nice, so had the accolades. But now it was time to move on to the next phase, to bring the campaign to life and sustain it for the duration of the contract. There'd be more intensive labor to make sure it was handled exactly right. Long hours and more meetings with Aviator Airlines folks.

It was the kind of plum assignment I had been working for and dreaming of. So what was the problem now?

I didn't share those thoughts with Micah as he drove me home, but he knew me well enough now to know that concerns were swirling beneath my upswept hairdo.

He pulled into the driveway when we reached my mother's house and turned toward me.

"So what's the problem? Your leave of absence has begun, and it's paid, mind you. Whenever you return to work, you'll have a prestigious account to handle. Why the long face?"

I didn't answer right away. This was usually the point in our conversation where I told him part of the truth but not all of it.

But tonight needed to be a turning point. Micah had seen me in my glory. If we were going to be more than just friends, I needed to introduce him to the real me to see if that's who he wanted to hang around with, or if he was only interested in the image I had created.

I looked into his eyes and began speaking softly and slowly.

"I've spent the past few years pushing myself to be the best ad woman I could be, to excel in this field and be at the top of my game. Part of it was because I like winning. I like doing my best at whatever I decide to pursue.

"But another reason I've been so driven, to the detriment of my weight and my devotion to God and even to the people around me like Tawana, is because I've been running from my demons."

Micah sat expressionless, patiently hearing me out. I took a deep breath and continued. What was he going to think of me, of my mother?

"I found out almost six years ago that the man I had been raised to believe was my father was really just the man whose name was on my birth certificate. My mother had an affair with a married man who is now one of the leaders of our church. She was also married at the time, and her husband, who I thought was my father, was killed by a drunken driver when I was eight months old. I don't know if he ever knew the truth. Mama told me just before I went to graduate school in Boston.

"So I'm really not a Jasper; that's just what was convenient for my mother to put on my birth certificate. I'm illegitimate. And my real surname has to be a secret to protect all parties involved."

Tears coursed down my cheeks as I continued. Micah's expression hadn't changed. He reached for my hands, but I pushed him away. He needed to know everything.

"There's more," I said, trying to compose myself. "Mama told me the truth because apparently my *real* father was feeling some sort of guilt and wanted to begin contributing more fully to my education. And to be honest, I didn't give her a chance to explain if she had other reasons for finally sharing her secret.

"But on the night she told me the truth, I basically cut her off. I stopped talking to her, stopped spending time with her or even acknowledging her presence. I went off to grad school and saw her only twice during that time, when I had to come home for breaks. She hasn't received a Mother's Day card from me since then.

"But even worse, the night Mama told me, I also took it out on God. I don't know if I blamed him, but I stopped praying and studying my Bible and going to church. The church was the house of hypocrites, as far as I was concerned.

"And I guess I felt like, what good could God do me if the person I trusted most, my mother, could do something so sinful and then lie to me about who I was for my entire life? I just wanted to wash my hands of everything. And so I did.

"At some point, I began trying to fill the emptiness inside with my work. That's how I have risen through the ranks at Turner One so quickly. I knew I couldn't change my past, but I was in control of the rest of my life. If I shaped that properly, then maybe my past wouldn't matter so much.

"But you know what, Micah? It has always mattered. Even though you're the first person I've ever shared this with, I've lived secretly with shame and with the pain of having a father so near yet unwilling to own me publicly."

I had looked down at my hands in my lap as I talked. Now I raised my eyes to Micah again to see if he were disgusted. His expression hadn't changed, but his eyes seemed softer.

"I came home to Mama to help her because I love her, but also because I feel so guilty. And at the same time, I'm still angry with her. She hasn't told me why she handled things the way she did. I'm still so hurt and ashamed. I just can't reconcile it all."

I finally sat silent and returned my gaze to my hands in my lap. I was afraid to hear what Micah would say. Or even worse, I figured he'd say the right things and then never call me again.

He leaned over and kissed my cheek. He used a thumb to wipe away the tear streaks there.

"Here bring your wounded hearts. Here bring your anguish. Earth has no sorrow that heaven cannot heal."

Micah recited the words to a song I hadn't heard in a long time.

"That's what God is always telling us, no matter how dark and ugly and terrible we think our sin is. You hurt God by distancing yourself from him, Serena, but who did you hurt more? What did you lose by turning away from God instead of turning to him when you needed him the most?"

I looked at Micah and whispered, "I lost myself."

"And as far as you being illegitimate, there is nothing illegitimate about you. No baby that's innocently born into this world should have to bear that label. And besides, think about how Jesus must have felt.

"He wasn't so-called illegitimate, of course, but half of Nazareth thought he was conceived out of wedlock. Mary and Joseph probably had to take a lot of stuff, what with people gossiping about her being pregnant before they got married and questioning whether the baby was his."

I laughed out loud at the mental picture Micah painted.

"And the biggest gossips were probably Mary's friends in the church!" I said.

Micah nodded and chuckled.

"Yep," he said. "The church is filled with wounded souls wounding others. We go there not because we're perfect, but because we need to be healed. So let's get real.

"You think all these folks around you have perfect lives? You think having the names on your birth certificate match the names of the people who raised you makes life any less difficult? Or makes you a better person?"

Before I could respond, he put a finger to my lips to silence me.

"I know, I know: I'm being too simplistic," he said. "This is really all about who you are; about you being able to trust in the place you've always thought you came from. If your mother could lie about something so important, how can you trust her or, for that matter, ever forgive her, right? How can you reconcile the pain of growing up fatherless with the fact that all along, your father sat in church with you, raising another family?"

I dissolved in tears as he spoke aloud the issues I had struggled with for so long.

"It sounds like you've asked these questions of yourself for too long by yourself," Micah said. "This secret is only harmful and shameful if you let it be.

"You aren't the only one ever conceived in this kind of circumstance, Serena. And guess what? You didn't have any say in the matter. If people want to judge you because of what your parents did, then they are petty and unworthy of your friendship anyway.

"But right now, you've been given the gift of time. You can use it to step back from work and determine what role that job will play in your life in the future. If you continue to oversee the Aviator Airlines account, for example, you'll need to figure out how to do it without putting in twelve-hour days all the time.

"Now is also the time to reconcile with your mother. You've got to talk to her about this. You've got to be honest with her.

"And you know what else? You've got to be real with yourself. You are a talented and beautiful young lady who grew up fatherless but turned out wonderful, Serena Jasper. The experiences you've had have helped make you who you are. You can use them to God's glory.

"You have nothing to be ashamed of, Serena. Only you can determine whether to own shame anyway, or to move forward with the truth in a way that strengthens you. Either way, you're not getting rid of me."

He kissed me lightly on the lips and then leaned across me to open my door.

The look in his eyes made mine misty.

I wanted to say more, but instead, I said good night. I knew he was sending me into the house to take care of business, whenever and however I saw fit. He knew the real Serena Jasper, and he hadn't run away. For the first time in a long time, my heart smiled.

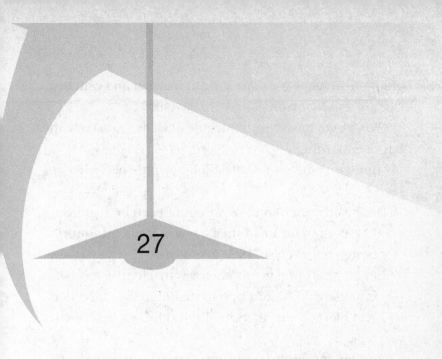

27

The way Mama gazed at me sometimes made me laugh. She acted like I was a newborn whose features she was getting to know for the first time.

"I'm just so happy you're here, baby," she'd say and smile when I questioned her stares. "It's been a long time."

The cancer treatments often left her weak and sick to her stomach. The little hair she'd had left after the first round of chemo was beginning to fall out, and she seemed to be losing more weight each day.

Mama had never been a heavy woman, but now she seemed almost frail. It broke my heart sometimes to watch her. But inside that shell was the same feisty woman with the same strong spirit.

Now that I didn't have to dash to work each morning, we had developed a comfortable routine of rising every day and taking a short walk down the block, if she felt up to it, and eating a light breakfast of mixed fruit or whole-grain cereal while we shared the newspaper and watched Charlie and Diane on *Good Morning America*.

"You've got me acting like a little old lady," I joked with her one morning.

"Hmmph," she'd said. "Best-looking little old lady I've seen."

The healthy diet and low-intensity exercise had been good for both of us. I had shed a few pounds without really trying, but even so, I felt much better.

Just being around my mother was making me feel better. In my anger, I hadn't permitted myself to miss her, so I had blocked out the joy of the times we had spent together.

I was grieving now for the little things I had missed, like how even now she still called me her "bambina" and kissed my forehead when she felt mushy, or how she could often tell what I was thinking before I uttered a word.

We focused on the happy memories and tried to have fun together. When Mama was sick, I held her hand or dabbed her forehead with a wet cloth. Often I would sit beside her bed while she slept. She would sometimes wake and smile when she found me there reading a book or magazine.

Neither of us had wanted to mar this bonding period with mention of the one remaining issue between us. It hovered over us like a cloud, though. One that for now, we could choose to ignore.

Today we were going to the hair salon and picking up our dresses for Imani's wedding the next day. Mine was at the bridal shop with the other bridesmaid dresses, and

Mama's department-store find was being altered at a local tailor shop to fit her shrinking frame.

I was hoping Mama wouldn't be too tuckered out by the time we finished our errands. I had made the hair appointments with Kirkland as early in the morning as I could, so we'd be the first in and out. He didn't disappoint me.

We both emerged looking better than ever after three hours in the salon, especially Mama, who had Kirkland style a new wig for her to wear to the wedding. It nearly matched the texture of her hair that had fallen out, and it was the same deep black her hair had been before beginning to turn gray.

As I gave her a once-over, I silently prayed for her.

"Lord, let her own hair grow back longer and more beautiful than ever. Let her see how truly beautiful she is right now, even with this illness, even as you send your healing."

She caught me staring at her through the mirror and turned toward me.

"What is it?"

I smiled. "Just admiring your beauty, that's all."

With more of our relatives in town for Imani's wedding, Mama had plenty of people to keep her company. I felt comfortable being out and about most of the day, running last-minute errands for Imani and for myself.

Imani's college roommate, Elaine, had helped me host a bridal shower the evening before for all of Imani's girlfriends who were just getting into town. I needed to deliver the gifts she had received to her parents' house. I also decided to stop by Tawana's and see how she and my cousin Tia had been faring.

Tia had eagerly stepped in as the Lamaze coach and was trying to be there for Tawana as much as she could. But I didn't want Tawana to think I was trying to get rid of her. I intended to be there for her and the baby too. I wanted to tell her that in person. I hoped she would believe me.

I climbed the stairs to the second floor of Tawana's apartment building and encountered a putrid smell just as I reached the landing. I held my breath for as long as I could, but I *had* to inhale some air, no matter what that dead, foul-smelling thing was in the corner!

Thinking about Tawana, and soon her baby, having no choice but to live here made me heartsick.

I turned and walked down the short hallway to Tawana's apartment. There was no need to knock tonight. Ms. Carson stood holding a bag of groceries in the narrow doorway and fumbling through her worn gray purse to find her keys.

"Hi, Ms. Carson," I said. "Let me take that for you."

I reached for her bag so she could search for the key. Ms. Carson gave me a once-over, taking in my jeans and green-and-white knit top and manicured nails before turning to open the door.

"Don't you have more important places to be?" she asked with contempt, turning her back to me as she opened the door and entered.

"What do you mean?" I asked. "Tawana is important."

Ms. Carson didn't invite me in, but I entered the apartment behind her and set the bag of groceries on the table in the tiny kitchen. I glanced over at the sofa but didn't see Tawana.

"Hmmph," Ms. Carson said grumpily. "She's important

all right. So important that I just used the last of my check to buy prenatal vitamins for Tawana and buy the noodles she eats while she's here all day, waiting for this baby to be born. I don't know why that girl had to go out and get herself a baby. Ain't nothing going to become of either of them!"

Ms. Carson slammed the cabinet door shut after she had stored her few groceries. She sat at the kitchen table and removed her shoes. A scowl remained on her face. "And I don't know why you and that other girl keep wastin' your time coming over here. You're big-time! Why don't you stay on over in the big-time part of the city with your big-time friends and stop coming over here to help a charity case? My daughter made this bed—now she's got to lie in it."

Anger surged through me, but I knew that now wasn't the time to lose my temper. I sat there silently for a few minutes, praying that God would take away the ugly feelings I had for this woman and infuse me with some of his divine love. I needed it right now so I wouldn't say the wrong thing and get kicked out.

Before I could reply, Tawana waddled into the room. Her expression didn't reveal whether she'd heard the resentful words spewing from her mother's mouth, but as she looked from her mother to me, I saw that she recognized her mother's foul mood.

"Hi, Serena," she said softly. "See how big I'm getting? Tia says the baby won't wait too much longer. I've already dropped."

I smiled at her anticipation. I could see that the baby was sitting lower in her uterus.

211

Ms. Carson slammed her hand on the table and glared at her daughter.

"You talkin' like this is something to be excited about. Who's going to feed the baby when it gets here? You? You shoulda thought about that, Tawana, before you went and lay down with some no-good man. Your father was no-good, all of these men around here are, so why did you even get into that? Why did you fall for his line? I thought you had a little common sense. Now you got this baby on the way, and your future is out the window!"

Ms. Carson yelled as I watched in horror. I hoped it didn't show on my face.

"You know what? When that baby is born, don't expect me to take it into my arms and take on a second job." She flung her arm toward me as she stomped to her bedroom. "Better yet, let Miss Thang handle it!"

The door slammed behind her, rattling the few pictures nailed to the wall. Tawana began to cry.

I led her to the sofa and sat beside her, putting my arm around her shoulders. "Calm down, T," I said, trying to soothe her. "Your mother's just tired. She's home early from work, so she must have had a bad day."

Tawana shook her head as the tears continued to fall.

"Any day she's in this house with me is a bad day for her!" she spat.

I sighed and looked up. *Lord?*

Tawana looked straight ahead but focused on nothing in particular as I gently rubbed her back.

"You know she's right, don't you? Everything my mama said was true," Tawana said, her voice void of emotion, just like her eyes. "I feel like I'm dying inside, right this very moment. My mouth works, I can talk. My heart is beating, I'm breathing in and out, but I'm dying."

Her despair seemed to fill the air.

"Tawana, listen to me." I turned the girl's shoulders toward me so she would be forced to face me. "Look at me."

Tawana looked up, her expression still blank.

"You made a choice, and your consequence is becoming a mother at too young an age. That does *not* mean your life is over. That does *not* mean you will never be loved.

"Sometimes our decisions land us in situations that aren't easy to handle, or that seem wrong to the world, or that just turn our whole lives upside down! But sweetheart, God loves you so much.

"I know you're having a hard time right now. But I'm here, T. God put us together for a reason. And most importantly, you have him to lean on. You don't even have to get on your knees. Just pray to him when you need him, and he will provide everything you need. Everything."

I held Tawana close and let the girl sob on my shoulder.

I realized that the lecture I'd given her echoed the one Micah had recently given me. Was I the pot calling the kettle black or what? But I knew that God could use me, in spite of my broken places, to help someone else.

Tawana finally composed herself enough to ask a question.

"How can I believe in a God I can't see, a God who has let me suffer this much pain?"

"Tawana, it's not his job to take away the pain, to make your life all rosy. The point is, he's going through the pain with you. And so am I, and so is my cousin Tia. We're here for you. Consider us dispatched by God. Not angels, unfortunately, but ladies who have your back."

She wiped her eyes with the back of her sleeve and smiled.

"You're funny when you try to talk hip."

I laughed.

"Are you trying to tell me that I'm old? Girl, I am all that and a bag of chips *with* dip!"

I rubbed her growing tummy.

"And I *am* here for you. Don't worry."

28

An *Essence* magazine cover model couldn't have been more beautiful.

Imani glided down the aisle on the arm of her father, beaming at her soon-to-be husband. John couldn't hold back the tears. He mopped his face with his handkerchief as Imani came toward him.

I glanced at Mama, who sat on the third row dabbing at her eyes. She had been sick that morning but had insisted on coming to the wedding.

"The only way I'm missing Imani's big day is if they take me out of here on a stretcher," Mama had said defiantly when I suggested she stay home and rest.

I knew when I was outdone. Mama was still Mama. She had the final say.

And I saw Erika and Elliott sitting across the aisle from Mama, holding hands and smiling at the bride. They looked like a happy young couple in love. I hoped things had gotten better.

Since I had moved out, Elliott had moved in, for all intents and purposes. Whenever I called, he answered the phone and offered lame excuses for why Erika couldn't talk. She and I hadn't touched base in the month since I had been at Mama's.

She called me from work a few times, but I was out buying groceries or taking Mama to her chemotherapy or radiation treatments. We needed to talk, though. I wasn't going to continue paying my part of the rent if Elliott had decided to become her new roommate.

As Imani neared the altar, Erika looked toward me and smiled. I winked at her before giving my cousin my full attention.

I took Imani's flowers so she could turn toward John and recite her vows. She looked angelic in the white satin beaded gown she had me try on for her first fitting.

Thankfully, I hadn't thrown anything off. Since we were about the same height and build, I'd been helpful enough for the seamstress to stay on track. The sleeveless gown with a fitted waist and flowing train was made for Imani.

As I had helped her dress, I teased her, "Since I've already worn it once, you'll let me borrow it when I need it, right?"

She laughed. "Who knows? Reverend Micah might have plans for you sooner than you think."

I had stopped applying her makeup and given her one of those "What you talkin' about?" looks. Micah hadn't come with me today because he'd gone home to Oklahoma to visit his parents for the weekend.

"What is up with you and my mother?" I asked Imani. "First you're her spy, keeping her informed about my promotion and all, and now she's yours? When did she tell you about Micah?"

The bride had waved me off with the hand bearing her sparkling engagement ring. "I can't get into all the details just now. But I know he's a keeper, and I'm praying for you two. And I just want you to know, I'm so happy you and Aunt Vi have worked things out."

She had smiled sweetly and handed me her shoes to slide on her feet while Aunt Jackie adjusted her veil on her head.

And now, after they finished their vows and her groom kissed her tenderly, he helped Imani turn toward their guests to be introduced as Mrs. John Davidson.

The applause was thunderous, and more than a few people shed tears of joy for them, including me.

Behind the happy couple, the other attendants and I glided down the aisle in our fitted sage green dresses, with the groomsmen just behind us.

Mama didn't rise to her feet, but from her seat she raised her hands above her head and clapped. She sat there for nearly an hour as the wedding photographer snapped pictures after the ceremony. She smiled and chatted with friends and relatives who wanted updates on how she was doing. She answered their questions and thanked them for their prayers, but kept steering the focus back to Imani.

"I appreciate you asking, but let's not dwell on me today," I heard her say more than once. "This is Imani and John's day. I don't want to dampen it with talk of doctors and medicine and the like. Let's watch the photo session."

As the bridal party gathered belongings and prepared to dash over to the reception in the Green Room of the Landmark Theatre, I felt a hand rest on my elbow. I turned around smiling, expecting to see a familiar face. I did, but this one caught me off guard.

Melvin Gates stood there, looking a bit nervous.

"Serena, how are you? I haven't seen you in a while. You're looking lovely as usual."

I stared at him but didn't speak. For the first time, I realized I had his full lips. But did he think after all this time he could just appear and strike up a conversation like nothing had changed? My mother had raised me not to be rude, but this was one of those times I was going to use the "I'm grown up" rule and make my own decision.

I reached for my bag with the clothes I had worn to the church and brushed past the good deacon without uttering a word.

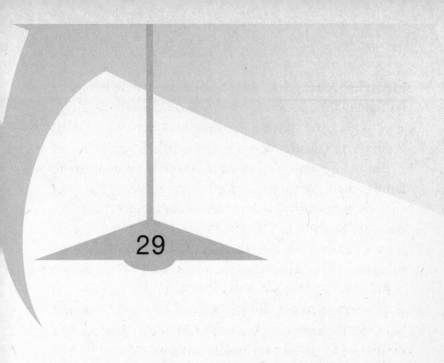

29

Mama, who was standing in the foyer of the church, saw the exchange.

As I strode toward her to tell her I'd pull my car up to the front of the church and pick her up, I could tell she wasn't pleased. But she also looked ill.

With her lips pressed together, she said, "Hurry up and get the car, Serena. I'm getting a little tired."

"Mama, are you in pain?"

She shook her head no, but her eyes revealed the truth. I knew she was trying to be strong because she didn't want me to skip Imani's reception.

"I just need to go home and lie down. I'll be fine. Hurry so you can drop me off and get to the reception. You're the maid of honor; you're needed there."

If she hadn't been right, I would have stayed home with her. Instead, after I got her settled on the sofa with a cup of tea and the remote control, I called our neighbor and

Mama's good friend, Miss Mary, to come sit with her while I attended the reception. She came over promptly.

"I'm glad you called. I'd love to stay here with Violet. We haven't talked in a while."

But by the time we walked from the front door to the family room, Mama had drifted to sleep.

"Don't you worry, Serena," Miss Mary said. "I'll sit here with her and watch TV or read a little until you return. Have a good time at the reception. I'll call you if any little thing comes up, I promise."

I hugged her. "Thank you, Miss Mary. Thank you."

The reception was lovely. But soon after I made my toast to the happy couple and watched their first dance, I whispered in Imani's ear that I had to go.

"You know I understand, CeCe," she had said and hugged me. "Thanks for everything. You've been wonderful. I love you."

"Back at you, Mrs. Davidson," I said and grinned, trying not to cry again.

I returned home to find Mama and Miss Mary shooting the breeze about their favorite soap stars.

"I tell you, that Erika Kane is something else," Miss Mary said and shook her head, as if talking about a real person. "She's had more husbands than cats have lives."

Mama chuckled.

"What about my man John Newman, on *The Young and the Restless*? He can't settle down either. Every time I think he and Nicki are going to work things out, something goes wrong. None of them is satisfied for long."

They turned when they heard me giggling.

"If I didn't know you two were talking about soap stars,

I'd think these were people you actually knew with these problems," I said.

"Hmmph, it's a lot like real life if you ask me," Miss Mary said. "I might not know an Erika Kane or a John Newman, but there are more than enough folks with those same issues to go around."

When Miss Mary left, Mama came to the table to eat the plate of food I had brought her at Aunt Jackie's insistence from the reception.

"So what was that about, at the church earlier?"

I had figured she'd use this time to talk to me about dissing Deacon Gates.

"What do you mean?"

I got up from the table and walked to the sink to begin washing the breakfast dishes. Before she became ill, Mama would have had a fit about me leaving dirty dishes in the sink. Now, she took that and a lot of other things in stride.

"The dishes can wait, Serena. Come talk to me."

I slid into the seat across from her and looked her in the eyes with as much defiance as I could muster. Even if she was sick, she deserved to know that I was still angry about the whole situation.

"What is there to say, Mama? For twenty-four years he knew he was my father while I didn't know, and he wants to come up to me today and say hello like nothing has changed between us?

"Should I have politely chitchatted with him? I don't think so. What I wanted to say is 'Thanks for nothing. Thanks for letting me watch you raise your beautiful family while I longed for a father of my own.'

221

"I wanted to thank him for making me feel like an outcast, an unwanted piece of trash when I finally learned the truth. If he were a real man, he would have approached me years ago after I called him and told him I knew. He would have at least apologized and tried to explain things to me. But he didn't.

"So he had no right to come sidling up to me at my cousin's wedding as if I were a long-lost family friend and tell me he wanted to say hello."

Mama paused after I finished, then took a bite of her roast beef.

"Was that meant for me too?" she asked.

I didn't know how to respond. She was sick; I didn't want to upset her.

The truth will set you free . . .

I took a deep breath and leaned in closer to grasp her hands.

"Yes, Mama, I guess it was meant for you too. I've been angry since you first told me. I've felt ashamed and misled. I've felt like the life you crafted for me when I was a child and the stories you told me about how good a person my father was were all convenient lies. What made you eventually tell me truth?"

If we were finally going to talk about it, I wanted to know.

"I decided to tell you then because Deacon Gates was doing well in the stock market and apparently had set aside some money to help with your education. He really wanted to pay for grad school, like I told you that night," Mama said. "He wanted me to tell you that an anonymous donor had provided the money, or that I had applied for some scholarships on your behalf. But I knew that it was time to stop lying. You were an adult. You had a right to know."

Mama looked at me earnestly and took both my hands in hers.

"I didn't tell you earlier, Serena, for a variety of reasons, most of them excuses to keep the pressure off myself. First, I felt like you were too young to understand. Then, when you hit adolescence, I didn't want to make your teenage years any more confusing than they had to be. And since Deacon Gates hadn't told his family, I knew it would be awkward for you to be attending high school with his two sons and not be able to share your kinship with them."

I interrupted. "Would it have been better if I had wound up dating one of them, Mama? I almost did!" I said bitterly.

She continued calmly. "You have a right to be angry, baby. I was wrong. We both were wrong."

"So why didn't you tell me when I graduated from high school?"

She looked toward the ceiling and took a deep breath.

"I really have no reason, other than I was scared of what you'd think of me, Serena. I was scared that you'd hate me.

"But I felt like I had to tell you when you got accepted to BU. I didn't want you to start your future hampered by thousands of dollars in student loans that needed to be paid off. Deacon Gates didn't either. We both felt it was the right time."

I stood up and walked to the sink. I peered out of the window into the backyard. "Mama, it sounds to me like it was all about the money at that point. It really wasn't about telling me the truth for truth's sake. I wouldn't be paying back loans now if I had heard you out and accepted the deacon's checks, right?"

"If I had known it would cost me you, Serena, I wouldn't have done it."

I turned to face her again. "But don't you see, Mama? That means I'd still be living a lie today. I needed to learn the truth, but not just because you were looking for a way for me to avoid student loans. It was just wrong."

"You're right, baby," she said softly. "I'm sorry for lying to you all of those years and for finally telling you the truth when I thought it would benefit both you and me. And I'm sorry you had to find out this way that your mother isn't perfect."

I pulled a chair close to her and sat down. "What happened, Mama? Weren't you and Deacon Gates both married?"

She looked upward, as if asking God how to go on.

"We were both married and both active in church and both well respected. And at the same time, we were both having problems in our marriages.

"We served together on St. Mark's treasury board, counting the offering on Sundays after service and after other programs held during the week. There were teams of three, and Deacon Gates and I happened to be on a team together with an older woman named Joan Marshall.

"The longer we worked together, the closer we became as friends. He'd confide in me sometimes when he and his wife had a bad fight, and I'd share my concerns about Herman being so distant.

"Herman lived with me and paid the bills, but he wasn't there with me. It was like I was his roommate, but his heart was somewhere else. I didn't know if he was having an affair or just didn't care about me anymore or what. But I was hurt and lonely a lot, even though I was married."

She paused and took my hand.

"I hope when you find that special person, the two of you will never drift apart like that, Serena. Marriage takes work, and the two of you must never forget that. When one person starts taking the relationship for granted, the other person gets resentful about picking up all the slack, and things begin to go sour.

"I'm not sure what the issues were in Deacon Gates's marriage, and I know now that it doesn't matter. Our decision to turn to each other instead of to our spouses and a counselor, or even to our pastor for prayer, was wrong.

"But that's what happened. Mrs. Marshall missed a lot of counting sessions with our team because her husband had a stroke. That meant Deacon Gates and I worked alone together a lot. What started out as friends confiding in each other led to us consoling each other.

"We were together twice, Serena, and it didn't feel right either time. I knew it was wrong. I went to the altar and prayed for forgiveness. But how could God forgive me if I kept committing adultery?

"So I quit the treasury board and told them I'd be busy on Sunday afternoons after church helping a family member."

I looked at her oddly. "So you lied to cover up an adulterous relationship?"

"That's how circles of lies start, baby. One lie leads to another," Mama said.

I remembered my advice to Erika months earlier to tell a fib to get out of attending a dinner hosted by Elliott's law firm. She had refused to lie, though it meant going late and being punished by Elliott afterward.

"But technically, I didn't lie," Mama explained. "I did take time on those Sundays to go by your great-grandmother's house and take her dinner and visit for a while. It was what I should have been doing all along.

"Grandma Rose was a wise old lady. And she knew Herman better than anyone else in the family. She could see how hurt I was by his indifference to me and our marriage. She told me she'd pray, but she also gave me practical suggestions on how to save my marriage, if I wanted.

"I never told her about my affair, but I think she suspected both Herman and I had been 'dippin' in other honey pots,' as she put it. I don't know if Herman was, but when we found out six weeks later that I was pregnant with you, after seven years of marriage and five years of trying to conceive, Herman didn't ask any questions.

"Even when you were born and looked nothing like him, Herman didn't question me. He knew we hadn't been intimate much during the time I conceived. He knew that I'd stayed out late a couple of nights. But when he held you, he fell in love.

"And I believe if he had lived, he would still love you today, Serena. Even if the truth had come out."

Mama sat back in her chair and sighed, as if a burden had been lifted off her shoulders.

"So he never knew I wasn't his daughter?"

Mama smiled. "If he knew, he didn't say anything. For all intents and purposes, you were his daughter, baby. He loved you with his whole heart. And before he died, he began to love me again too. So all those good things I told you about him weren't lies. Somehow we found our way back to each other before he died. I'm so thankful for that."

"And you never told him about your affair?"

"I tried to a few times, but he never let me finish. I don't think he wanted to know. He knew that he had pushed me away, and I guess he figured he bore some responsibility for anything that may have happened during that time.

"I followed his lead," Mama said. "I asked God to forgive me for my sins and to help me forgive Herman for anything he had done that was detrimental to our relationship. I asked God to heal my heart and transform me into the woman he'd have me to be.

"That prayer didn't make me perfect, Serena, as you've found out. But it made me a better person than I was before."

I nodded. "I understand what you're saying, Mama. But I still have questions. Did Deacon Gates ever ask about me? Did he wonder if I were his baby? What about his wife?"

"Deacon Gates knew without me telling him that you were the little girl he and his wife had longed for years to have. He called me from his job the Monday after he'd seen you at church to tell me how beautiful you were.

"But there was an immediate, unspoken understanding. You were my daughter and Herman's daughter. He never referred to you as his. If his wife suspected something, she never said anything to me.

"Deacon Gates kept his distance until your father died. Then every so often, he'd send me a little money in the mail to help you out. He helped pay for your high school graduation party and for your car. It wasn't much, but every little bit helped."

More secrets. I had been oblivious to them.

But what more could I say? Where was anger going to get me at this point? Mama admitted she had made a mistake—what more could I ask of her?

"So why do you think Deacon Gates tried to talk to me today?"

Mama looked puzzled. "Maybe he wanted to see how you'd react, if you'd play along with the ruse. Or maybe he really wants to get to know you, Serena. I really can't say. We still go to the same church, but we stay out of each other's way. I shake his hand sometimes when I pass the offering plate; otherwise, we don't communicate much.

"But even as I sit here, ashamed as I recount the mistakes I've made, I can't say that I'd change history, because then I wouldn't have you. Do you understand? I'm not saying you're the result of my sin. You're the gift God gave me in spite of my sin."

I hugged her. "Thank you for that, Mama. I needed to hear that."

"You're welcome, baby. I meant it."

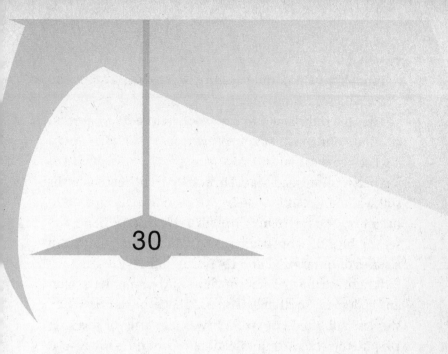

30

awoke with a start to find a white-bearded man standing over me.

"Ms. Jasper? Sorry to wake you."

He gave me a few seconds to orient myself. I sat up
straighter in the uncomfortable chair and stifled a yawn. I
was at the Medical College of Virginia Hospital, in Mama's
intensive care unit room.

Dr. Berry was making his morning rounds. He had gently
touched my forearm to wake me.

"Did you sleep in that chair all night? We'll have to make
sure they get you a cot."

I took that statement as a sign that Mama wouldn't be
leaving the unit anytime soon.

"How is she, Doc?" I asked.

He didn't smile.

"Do you have any other family you want present as I
share my diagnosis?"

I shook my head and tried not to tremble.

God, please save my mama.

That prayer formed in my mind before he offered to continue our conversation elsewhere.

"Let's go outside," he said.

The morphine had Mama in a deep sleep, but the doctor still wanted to talk privately. We rode the elevator up to his office, and he led me through a side door. When I was seated, he pulled out Mama's chart and began pointing to a series of ultrasound and CAT scan films.

"These are the most recent views of your mother's colon and abdomen. See that dark mass? That's the cancer. When she was admitted last week, it was a quarter of this size. Despite the chemo and radiation, it continues to grow. It appears to have spread to her bones."

He put down the chart and looked me in the eyes. "Ms. Jasper, there's nothing more we can do now but make your mother comfortable. I'm sorry."

I bowed my head to my chest and pursed my lips, trying to stifle the sobs.

This man was delivering a death sentence.

What about my prayers? And the prayers of our church, our family, and our friends?

I looked up but couldn't see Dr. Berry's face for my tears. "How much longer?" I managed to whisper.

He shook his head.

"To be honest, I don't know with certainty. But I doubt if she'll leave the hospital. She's not healthy enough for us to send her home or to recommend hospice care. She needs oxygen and high doses of morphine to stay comfortable."

"Will she continue to sleep all day and night, or will I have a chance to talk to her again?" I asked.

He pondered the question.

"The morphine keeps her dazed. But I understand your need for some closure. Just for today, I'll ask the nurses to cut her dosage enough to allow her to be lucid for some periods. But if she complains of being in too much pain, we'll have to up it again.

"Any other questions? I know I've given you a blow this morning. You're a young woman, to be handling this all on your own."

"I'm an only child, and my father is deceased."

I could say that now without flinching, after my talk with Mama a few weeks ago. I'd never known Herman Jasper, but he had loved me as his daughter. That was what mattered.

"I'll call my relatives and tell them to come. Thank you, Doctor, for being so candid."

He walked me back to Mama's room and gave me a hug. "Your mother has been a brave woman, Serena. Her faith has inspired me and the other doctors and nurses who have cared for her. Who knows how God decides whom to take and whom to leave here with us a little longer? I'm a doctor, and I don't know. But take comfort in the fact that your mother has lived well and touched many people. She's a good woman, and it's been a blessing to treat her."

He raised his palm. "And don't take these comments as a sign that I've given up on her. I'm still giving her whatever care is best for her at this point. I just wanted to share that with you while we're here right now."

Fresh tears formed in my eyes.

That almost sounded like a eulogy. I'm not ready for that. But will I have any choice?

I paged Micah as soon as I was back in the room.

He called right away.

"Serena? You need me there?"

I couldn't speak through my tears. My silence was his answer.

"I'll see you in fifteen minutes."

By the time he arrived, Pastor Taylor was there. Micah had called him immediately and asked him to join me at the hospital. Pastor had prayed with Mama and me and was talking with me softly when Micah pushed open the door.

I motioned for him to come on in. He was family; I didn't mind if he heard what Pastor Taylor was saying.

The two men shook hands. They knew each other from Union's seminary, where Pastor Taylor taught a few adjunct classes.

"Sorry to interrupt," Micah said softly. "I can excuse myself."

I shook my head. "No, please stay."

He stood beside me and held my hand as Pastor Taylor continued.

"As I was saying, we do believe that God can heal the body, mind, and spirit, Serena. He could heal your mother in this very instant if he wanted to. But sometimes he doesn't. Sometimes that's not part of his plan, and we don't know why.

"I'm not advising you to give up on a miracle, because with God anything is possible. But if it's time to let Violet go, then it's time. How do we discern that?

"Our prayers right now need to include fervent petitions for God's will to be done. If he wants your mother to stay on earth a little longer, so be it. If it's time for her to grace heaven, so be it."

Tears coursed down my cheeks as I nodded, recalling the sermon he had preached the Sunday I first learned of Mama's illness.

"It is well," I whispered. "It is well."

Micah squeezed my hand.

After another brief prayer, Pastor Taylor left. Micah told me he had called Imani in Washington and her parents, my aunt and uncle. They were going to alert the rest of the family, including my grandmother, about my conference with the doctor.

I stood to accept the hug he offered me.

"This is unreal," I said, sniffling. "This can't be happening. My mama is strong and vibrant and a fighter. I've been so focused on her beating this thing that I haven't considered the alternative. Micah, what if the doctor is right, that she won't go home? What am I going to do if she dies?"

He hugged me tightly. "We'll deal with whatever comes together."

My cell phone rang loudly from my purse in the corner. It hadn't done so in so long, I had forgotten it was there. I had been off work from Turner One for six weeks. And the hospital rule was to turn off all electronic devices.

The number was familiar. It was my cousin Tia's.

She sounded breathless when I called her back.

"Serena, Tawana has gone into premature labor. I'm dashing out of my office now, but by the time I make it downtown, she may have already had the baby. I hate to

233

bother you when you're with Aunt Vi, but can you try to meet Tawana in obstetrics? She sounded as if she were about to panic when I talked to her on the phone, and the ride in the ambulance has probably terrified her."

I didn't respond for a few minutes. I couldn't tell Tia on the phone that Mama was dying. I looked toward Mama, who was beginning to stir. I looked at Micah, whose eyes questioned me.

"Tawana's in labor and on her way here," I told him. "Tia's rushing over to help her with the baby but is afraid she won't get here in time."

He understood my anxiety.

"Tell her you'll go meet Tawana."

He saw the panic fill my eyes, and he grasped my shoulder before I could protest.

"Don't worry. I'll start praying the minute you leave that God won't take her while you're doing his will elsewhere," he said softly. "God is faithful."

I told Tia I'd find Tawana, and I urged her to stop by Mama's room. I hung up the phone and turned to find Mama staring at me.

"Hey, baby," she said in a near whisper.

Without her hair or her wig or the usual fullness of her face, she looked like a war refugee.

I leaned over and gently kissed her cheek.

"Hey, Mama, how you doing?"

"I'm hanging on," she answered slowly and honestly. "Did I hear you mention Tawana? Has she had the baby?"

"She's on her way here now, Mama. She went into labor early."

"Are you going to help her? Or is Tia here?"

I didn't want to leave, now that she was awake.

"Tia's on her way."

Mama frowned. "Until she gets here, you go be with Tawana. That girl loves you, and she needs you right now."

"And you don't?" I said with a mock attitude.

She looked me in the eyes. "I'm tired, but I'm not going anywhere right now, baby. Tawana needs you. Go."

My tears splattered on her cheek.

"What's all that for?" she said and tried to wipe one away. I did it for her.

"Mama, I love you so much. I'm sorry for the years I wasted, keeping you at bay. I wish I could get them back. I hope you can forgive me."

She grasped my hand as firmly as her frail strength would allow. "Serena, there's more than enough forgiveness to go around. Everything we've both been through has been worth it if the experiences have made us better people and better able to love others without judging them harshly.

"You use the truths about yourself to help others blossom. Don't be ashamed of who you are because of the mistakes I made. You are a queen, baby. One of God's children. He doesn't make mistakes, even when we do."

I turned to Micah when she said that and smiled through my tears. He smiled back through his own.

"You're stealing my lines, Ms. Jasper," he told her.

She looked at him and smiled. "Hi, handsome. I didn't even see you standing there. Come sit and talk to me while my daughter helps deliver a baby."

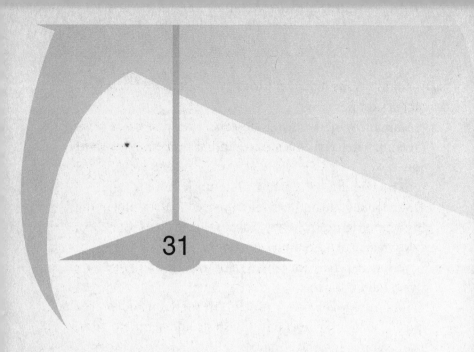

31

I found Tawana in tears and cowering on her cot in Labor and Delivery like a frightened kitten. I had to convince the nurses I was her labor coach before they'd let me in. Thankfully, I had accompanied her to a few doctor's appointments and had met her obstetrician.

Dr. Stephens recognized my name and cleared me to join Tawana. She wasn't due to deliver for another few weeks, but her water had broken, and it looked like the baby was on its way.

Relief washed over the teenager's face when she saw me.

"You came," she said and relaxed, allowing the nurses to lay her flat on the bed and hook her up to a machine that would permit them to monitor the baby's heartbeat.

"I'm here," I told her and hugged her. "Everything is going to be fine. Calm down and do what the doctor and nurses tell you to do. I'm with you every step of the way."

My thoughts briefly returned to the sixth floor, where Mama lay.

Lord, I trust you, I prayed silently. *Please let Mama hold on. I'm not ready to say good-bye yet. I need to be here for Tawana, but I don't want Mama to go without me there. Please, Lord, help her to hold on.*

Dr. Stephens slid latex gloves over her hands before positioning Tawana to check how much she had dilated. Her eyes widened, and she yelled for a nurse.

"Get everything ready! This baby is coming *fast*. She's already ten centimeters!"

Twenty minutes later, Tawana and I both were sweating.

Every time the doctor ordered her to push, I gripped her shoulders and urged her on. "You can do it, T. You can do it. Keep pushing! Push that baby out!"

Tawana folded her petite body forward. She released a piercing scream, one that under different circumstances might have propelled my heart through my T-shirt. But in this instance, I knew the cries were serving a purpose.

Seconds later, Tawana slumped into my arms, her sandy brown hair in disarray, eyes closed. A higher-pitched cry split the air. Dr. Stephens rose from the foot of the bed and brought a squalling infant to Tawana's side.

"Congratulations, Tawana," the doctor said. "You have a little girl."

She placed the bloody baby on the girl's chest for a few seconds before a nurse whisked the tiny infant away. Tawana sobbed. So did I.

I wasn't sure about her tears, but my tears were bittersweet.

Why, Lord, are you allowing me to help a life come into the world while at the same time taking one from me that means so much?

I couldn't understand it.

My ways are not your ways.

Come to me, and I will give you rest.

Where you are right now is where you're supposed to be.

I make no mistakes.

Everything is beautiful in its time.

My tears flowed more.

Yes, Lord, I said silently. *I hear you. I trust you.*

I hugged Tawana and kissed the girl's sweaty forehead. "You did good, sweetie. Real good," I said softly.

"Thanks," Tawana mumbled, tears still streaming from her eyes.

The awe of giving birth, coupled with the fear of what lay ahead, fueled the waterfall, I suspected.

"I couldn't have made it through this without you. You're like a big sister to me."

"*Like* a big sister," I said, feigning an attitude. "Young lady, I *am* your big sister. Always will be."

We smiled at each other before turning our attention to the little person squirming on the metal scale a few feet away. Misha continued to whimper as the doctor and nurse examined her.

"Five pounds, five ounces," the nurse called out as she began to diaper and dress the baby in a miniature T-shirt and knit hat.

"Hello, Misha," Tawana said and grinned.

I wanted to bask in the miracle I had just witnessed, but already, worry was dancing on the shoulders of my joy. More than a few miracles would be necessary for Tawana and Misha to have a decent life. I was determined to do what I could to make it happen, and I knew Tia would too.

I said a silent prayer that this infant wouldn't be Tawana's excuse to give up on life.

Just as the nurse placed Misha in Tawana's arms, the door swung open. Ms. Carson walked in wearing khaki slacks, a maroon shirt, and the once-white sneakers that served as her uniform at the plant. Her face was expressionless.

I looked at Tawana to gauge her reaction. It was guarded. Her eyes said she wanted to celebrate the arrival of this baby without being whiplashed by her mother's angry words.

Ms. Carson stood by the door, looking from Tawana to the blanket-swaddled baby for a few seconds before she spoke.

"I got here as fast as I could," she said as she slowly approached the bed. "It took me another fifteen minutes to convince the nurse down the hall that I had permission to come to your room. I'm sorry I missed her birth."

Tawana clutched Misha closer but didn't speak. I moved away from the bed, preparing to step outside while they visited.

"Don't go, Serena. Please stay," Tawana said.

Ms. Carson looked at me and nodded. She reached over the rail of the hospital bed and gently pulled back the cover surrounding Misha's face for a better look.

She spoke so softly that her broken voice was barely audible. "The day I gave birth to you was the happiest and the saddest day of my life. I was so happy to have someone

239

all my own to love. You were my own little doll, Tawana. But I was sad because I knew my having you so young probably meant I'd never leave the projects.

"Your father walked out on me the day I told him I was pregnant and never looked back. He had been my boyfriend for two years, and we were going to go off to college together and get married.

"When I got pregnant with you, Raymond pushed me out of his dream. He went on to college. I was trapped by motherhood and poverty."

Ms. Carson looked from Tawana to the baby. "I'm sorry I been so mean. I just didn't want that for you. It's a hard life. You know I've had to go on welfare sometimes to feed us. It's been embarrassing.

"But I did it because I loved you. And I tried to teach you that education, not boys, was your way out. Your way to a better life. Then you came home pregnant. At age sixteen, just like me. A baby girl, just like me. Stuck in the ghetto, just like me."

The words bitterly rolled off her lips. Her eyes didn't leave Tawana's face.

Tawana listened, wide-eyed at her mother's revelations.

"I'm sorry I let you down," Tawana said.

Ms. Carson held the palm of one hand to her forehead and placed the other hand on her hip, as if she were trying to come up with a solution. I realized, though, that she was finally accepting that her bitterness about the situation wasn't helping.

"I was so angry at you I couldn't look at you, Tawana. I felt like you had closed the door on a new beginning for our family. Because when you left the projects you were going to make something of yourself."

She looked up and into Tawana's eyes.

"You made mistakes just like I did, but you aren't trapped. I'm going to do what I can to help you make it."

She glanced toward me, over by the door to the room.

"I see you have other friends in your corner too."

I walked over to Ms. Carson and hugged her.

Misha began to squirm. Tawana awkwardly held her, trying to remember to support the infant's head like she had learned in the childbirth classes she had attended with Tia.

"Want to hold her?" she asked me and her mother.

Ms. Carson gestured toward me.

"She should go first," she told Tawana. "She helped you get her here."

I gingerly took the baby from Tawana.

Wrapped in a feathery-soft pink blanket with a matching cap, Misha puckered her miniature lips as if trying to talk or offer a kiss. Her dark eyes darted back and forth from one side of my face to the other, attempting to focus. Her face, flattened from childbirth, already resembled her mother's, especially the slanted eyes.

I nuzzled my nose against the baby's cheek and whispered, "Nice to meet you, Misha. We're going to get to know each other well."

And my tears flowed again. My heart was full of joy and heartbreak all at once.

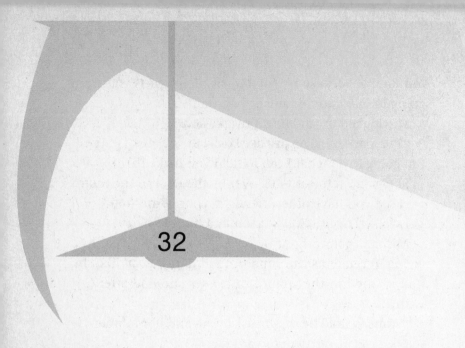

32

By early afternoon the next day, Dr. Stephens reluctantly agreed to let Tawana bring Misha down to Mama's room.

Even though Mama was drifting in and out of sleep, I knew she would be thrilled to meet the baby. I shook her shoulder gently when Tawana arrived sitting in a wheelchair pushed by a nurse. She clutched the tightly bundled Misha to her chest.

"Mama, you have a special visitor," I said when she opened her eyes.

She slowly turned her head toward Tawana and saw the baby.

"Oh, how precious," she said in the near-whisper she'd been speaking in all day. "Is this the baby you helped bring into the world, Serena? You've participated in a miracle."

Mama smiled at Tawana. "She's beautiful, sweetheart.

You just trust your mothering instincts, don't be afraid to seek help or advice when you don't know something, and love your baby always," she told the girl. "You'll make mistakes, but when you do, admit it.

"Tell her the truth, and you'll work through things together. And be sure to take care of *you*, Tawana. Get your education so you can do everything you need to do for your daughter. Godspeed to both of you."

That speech left Mama drained. She sighed deeply and rested her head on her pillow, trying not to be rude and fall asleep with Tawana still there. The nurse could see Mama's struggle. She said Misha had to get back to the nursery, into an incubator since her lungs were a little underdeveloped. Otherwise, she was a perfectly healthy baby.

"Thanks, Tawana, for bringing her down," I said. "I'll come by your room soon."

She balked at my promise to come by her room later. I could tell that the advice from my mother had touched her. Even she could see how sick Mama was.

"No hurry, Serena. I know you're here with your mother. You take your time," she told me. "Tia already brought us balloons and a camera to take pictures, and my mama came by before work with a teddy bear for Misha and clothes for me to wear home. I'll be okay. Misha and I will see you soon. We love you."

She waved good-bye as the nurse rolled her out of the room. Mama had lost her battle to stay awake and didn't acknowledge Tawana's departure.

When they were gone, Aunt Jackie and Gram were able to return from the waiting room. No more than three visitors were allowed in the room at one time. They had been at the hospital since yesterday, when I had gone to help Tawana deliver the baby. Micah had called them.

Aunt Jackie hugged me tightly. "That's a beautiful baby, Serena. I know you feel blessed to have witnessed her birth. How are you holding up?"

Today was going to be a lost cause in the composure department. The tears came again. I couldn't talk through them.

My aunt took me to a corner of the room, out of Mama's line of sight, and held me while I sobbed. She rubbed my head as I rested it on her shoulder.

"I *can't* do this," I cried. "I can't let her go. I won't have anybody. I'll be an orphan."

I sobbed more fiercely.

Aunt Jackie just held me. Eventually, she squeezed my arm to alert me that someone had entered the room. I mopped my face with my hands and turned around to find Erika there.

She ran toward me and embraced me. Her tears started mine to flowing again. Aunt Jackie nudged the two of us toward the door.

"I don't want Vi to wake up and get upset," she whispered.

Erika grasped my hand and led me out of the room, down the hallway to a quiet corner. She hugged me again and handed me a tissue from her purse.

"Micah called. Serena, I'm so sorry. Is the doctor sure? Have you gotten a second opinion?"

I couldn't bring myself to answer her questions. But I understood them. I wanted there to be an alternative to this too. But deep within, I knew nothing that any doctor said would matter now.

"She's in God's hands, Erika. Whatever he wills, will happen. There's nothing more the doctors can do. Our prayers are what matter now, and through them, God will accomplish his purpose."

I laughed dryly after I made the comments. "I sound so self-assured, so spiritual, don't I?" I said. "I'm uttering words that I hardly believe. My heart is shattering right now, but I'm sounding as if I've got it all together.

"Believe me, I don't. I'm just trying to be here for Mama and move in God's timing. I think this part stinks, mind you, but I can't change it, so I'm here."

She squeezed my hand. For some reason, I noticed her lavender, calf-length silk dress.

"You look pretty," I said as I wiped my eyes with the tissue. "What are you up to today?"

Her expression changed.

"I was going to surprise you and tell you when I got back, but you might as well know now. This isn't the best of times to share good news, but Elliott and I are leaving in a few hours for Jamaica. We're eloping."

My head whipped to the side as if I'd been slapped.

Who said this was good news?

Fortunately, the words that came to mind didn't leave my lips.

"Didn't you two just get engaged?" I finally said. "What happened to all the elaborate planning you were doing with the bridal magazines?"

She turned and walked toward the waiting room and

motioned for me to follow. When we had settled in a quiet spot, off to ourselves, she explained.

"I was busy planning everything, but Elliott decided last week that he wanted to scrap the big wedding and just go off and elope. He said it would be romantic and different," she explained, sounding as if she were still trying to convince herself this was the right thing to do.

"But Erika, as long as I've known you, you've talked about your dream wedding and finding the perfect dress to wear as you waltz down the aisle," I said. "This is a once-in-a-lifetime experience. Elope? Come on!"

She began to wring her hands. The stunning diamond Elliott had given her glistened.

"I know, I know," she said. "But Elliott recently learned that he's on the fast track to being made partner. He thinks it would help if we go to the law firm's annual meeting in Phoenix next month as husband and wife. It will show his stability and that he's ready to settle down and be a committed partner."

This shows stability? I thought. *On what planet?*

So much had occurred in the past two days that I felt like throwing my hands in the air and telling Erika "Whatever." This was her life. She could ruin it if she wanted.

But I couldn't send my friend on her way without trying to save her from herself, from this man who said he loved her.

I knew my words probably wouldn't change anything, but what if something happened to her and I hadn't uttered them? I loved her too much not to speak the truth.

"Erika, is this about you two being in love, or about him making a smart business decision? If they value him enough to consider him for partnership, surely the fact that you two are engaged would be enough to bolster his standing."

My frankness raised her defenses.

"We're going to use the money we'd have spent on a big wedding to buy a house. Elliott says we'll have to find something in just the right neighborhood after he becomes a partner. Every little bit will help.

"Besides, Serena, it really doesn't matter where we get married, just as long as we're husband and wife."

But it did matter, especially if the husband part of the equation was the only one who would be allowed to make decisions. I tried one more time.

"Erika, you are a strong black woman with so much going for you. You have a good heart. You're gorgeous. You could have your pick of successful, kind men. Yes, Elliott is good-looking, well-to-do, and on his way up. But any man that hits a woman is worthless, regardless of his credentials."

She flinched.

"I'm not trying to hurt you, Erika. I love you. I just don't want you to make a choice that could leave you bruised and battered, or even worse, for years to come."

I reached for her hand. "I've been running from my own truths for a long time. Now I know that no matter how far we run, the truth is our shadow. We can't change who we are or magically turn other people into who we want them to be. We have to accept ourselves. And we have to accept the faults and flaws in others too. But that doesn't mean we have to live with their faults.

"If Elliott loves you as much as he says, he'll get some

247

help and not push you into marriage until he has made some changes."

Tears began forming in her eyes. I could see fear and uncertainty there.

"I'm here for you, Erika, whatever you decide. I love you."

She squeezed my hand and smiled. I knew she hadn't changed her mind.

"I'm glad to know you'll love me even if you don't agree with my choices. I love Elliott, and he loves me. We can work through our issues together. He's already promised me that we will. He's my soul mate, Serena."

With those words, I released her into God's care.

I offered a hug.

"Still friends?" I asked.

She nodded and accepted my embrace.

"Always, Serena. Always."

We stood to walk back to Mama's room so Erika could spend some time with her. Before we reached Mama's door, Imani emerged.

When she saw me, she took my hand.

"I was coming to find you. Aunt Vi is awake," she said. "She's calling for you, Serena."

33

Rain pummeled the roof of the limousine. Was God weeping with me?

My eyes were dry at the moment, but the dam could burst any second now. As she had held me in her arms one last time, Mama had told me not to cry for her. She was going home to rest. She wasn't afraid, she said, but she would miss me.

"I know I've prepared you to go forward," she had said. "Walk in God's truth and love yourself, Serena. Listen to God when he speaks to you, and you'll make the right choices."

Memories of our final minutes together began to move me. I pulled a tissue from my purse. Micah offered his handkerchief.

"I'm fine," I told him as I dabbed at the corners of my eyes.

He and Imani, who sat on the other side of me, exchanged glances.

"No, you're not," she said. "And that's okay. You're saying a formal good-bye today, but your mother will always be part of you."

I nodded. "I feel her with me now."

After the eulogy, a childhood friend of Micah's approached the piano. Micah rubbed my hand.

When Smokie Norful launched into "I Need You Now," my favorite song off his first gospel CD, I closed my eyes and meditated on the words.

I stretch my hands to Thee. Come rescue me, I need You right away.

Those words captured how Mama felt when she left this earth, with me and our other relatives praying as we surrounded her bed. They also spoke for me at this moment. I would need God's help to endure the rest of this day and certainly the rest of the journey he'd take me on.

Later, as I sat on Mama's sofa and stared at a picture of her when she was about thirty, someone entered the living room and sat beside me. I looked up and found myself staring into Deacon Melvin Gates's eyes. He motioned toward the picture I was holding.

"I knew her then," he said of my mother. "We were friends about that time."

I waited for him to continue.

"We made some mistakes. But both of us moved on and went back home, not just physically, but with our hearts."

Deacon Gates stood and walked toward the fireplace, leaving his back toward me.

"I can't speak for Violet, but I know I never really recovered, because even though I asked God to forgive me, I never asked for *her* forgiveness."

He turned toward me but kept his head lowered.

"And to make matters worse, I never acknowledged you. I knew the first time I saw you that you were mine. I both loved and resented you. My wife and I had longed for a daughter and never had one, until we adopted Kami twelve years ago.

"And Herman doted on you, treating you like a Kewpie doll and the best thing since sliced bread. When he died, I felt terrible for you but selfishly thought at least another man wouldn't be raising my daughter."

He raised his eyes to gauge my reaction. I said nothing and tried to maintain my composure.

"You never knew this old deacon was so trifling, did you?"

I sighed heavily. "It doesn't matter, Deacon Gates," I said. "I've spent too many years feeling hurt and unloved because I believed I was nothing more to you than a shameful secret. And maybe I have been. But it doesn't matter anymore. Whether you acknowledge me as your daughter today or decide to never tell a soul, I'll be okay.

"My mother loved me deeply, and so did Herman Jasper, according to what I've been told. I don't have parents anymore, but I'm surrounded by people who care about me, so I'll eventually be all right."

He walked over and sat next to me again.

"I know I can never replace either of your parents, Serena, and I'm not asking to try. But if you'll allow me to, I'd like to at least attempt to be a better friend than I've pretended to be all of these years.

"I told my wife the truth last week, after Violet died. She had suspected it all these years but was hurt to find out it was true. Still, she's trying to forgive me and move on. I've asked her, and if you're willing, I'd like to include you in our family. I'd like to acknowledge you as my daughter and get to know you in that way, or in whatever way you choose."

I looked at him for the longest time without responding.

What could I say? My emotion had been spent today on burying my mother. There was nothing left.

But I remembered her words, to try to love others as I wanted to be loved and to try not to judge so harshly.

I didn't know if I wanted a relationship with Deacon Gates and his family. It wasn't a decision I was going to make lightly. I'd pray on it and try to discern what would be best for me.

But I appreciated his truth today and his willingness to let his defenses down so he could approach me. Finally, I answered him.

"I really don't know what I want or need right now, as far as a relationship with you, Deacon Gates. But thank you for coming here and opening your heart to me. I know it couldn't have been easy," I said. "I've got a lot of healing to do before I make any big decisions, and deciding to be publicly acknowledged as your daughter is a big decision.

"At the least, we can be friends. But I hope you'll give me the space to decide on what terms. Right now, that's all I can offer."

"I understand, Serena," he said solemnly. "You know

where to find me when, or if, you ever want to talk or if you need anything. I'm finally coming out of hiding."

I smiled gingerly at him.

"Me too, Deacon Gates," I said. "I'm finally owning and accepting Serena Jasper as she is."

Micah stood in the doorway of the living room and cleared his throat to let us know he was there.

"Sorry to interrupt," he said. "Serena, the last of the visitors are leaving. I thought you'd want to know."

Deacon Gates and I rose at the same time. I gave him a light hug.

"Thank you for coming. And for talking to me. It meant a lot. Really."

He nodded and took my hands in his.

"You're in my prayers," he said and left the room.

Micah came over to me, his eyes revealing concern. "Everything okay?"

I hugged him and rested my head on his chest. "Better than okay, Micah. God doesn't make any mistakes."

He looked down at me and smiled.

"You stole my line," he said softly. "We have to talk."

I laughed and took his hand as we walked into the foyer so I could say good-bye to Miss Mary and several other neighbors who had come to pay their respects. Aunt Jackie held the door open for them. I noticed the rain had finally stopped.

"Just a few minutes ago," she said when she realized what had garnered my attention.

Though it was almost nightfall and the sun tinged only a portion of the sky, I just knew Mama was going to ask God to send a rainbow.

acknowledgments

From the time I could comprehend words on a page, I knew I wanted to pen them. As Scripture says, "(God)has made everything beautiful in its time" (Eccles. 3:11).

One's dreams rarely become reality without the support of others. Given that, I humbly express my gratitude to those who have been so helpful to me.

I first thank God, my heavenly Father, for not only giving me this gift of writing but also for allowing me to use it in a way that brings his name honor. I thank my husband, Donald, for his belief in me and for always being so helpful with our little ones. I thank my two children for sharing Mommy with the computer and showering me with love.

I also extend gratitude to Dr. Bobbie Walker for her faith in my ability to write this book when it was just in the idea stage; to my fellow writers, Teresa Coleman, Otesa Middleton, and Sharon Shahid for reading the manuscript and offering candid and thoughtful insight; Michelle Oliver, Comfort Anderson-Miller, Robin Farmer, Phyllis Theroux,

Barbara Rascoe, Lee Knapp, Kyle Grinnage, Gwendolyn Richard, and Yolanda Young for an always available dose of encouragement; Muriel Miller Branch, my spiritual and writing mentor, for allowing God's Word for *her* to also inspire me; my mother, and my siblings, Dr. Barbara Grayson, Henry Haney, Sandra Williams, and Patsy Scott, for always cheering me on; my second set of parents, Earnett and Mae Evelyn Adams; my goddaughter Kourtney Cannon; and to my friends and family across the country who have blessed me with prayers and support over the years.

I extend a special thank-you to my editor, Brian Peterson, for reading this manuscript and believing in its potential; to my sweet friend Kim Newlen, for connecting me with Brian; to my agent, Pamela Harty; and to the wonderful editing and marketing team at Revell.

My hope is that this novel has not just entertained you but has also spoken to your hearts in a powerful way. I share it with each of you, and with other readers, from my heart.

Blessings,
Stacy

Stacy Hawkins Adams is an award-winning reporter and inspirational columnist for the *Richmond Times-Dispatch* in Richmond, Virginia. She also operates ClayWork Enterprises, a motivational speaking business. She and her husband, a minister, live in a suburb of Richmond with their two young children. This is her first novel. She welcomes readers to visit her website: www.stacyhawkinsadams.com.